KU-570-971

BITTER IS THE DUST

When Sarah McKinney finally escapes the clutches of her abusive husband, she and her adopted son Jason begin a perilous new life on the run. Eventually they settle down as Sarah finds work as a doctor's assistant, and Jason is reunited with his real father and takes a job as a ranch hand. But Jason's quick temper soon gets him into trouble with his employer, and their future hangs in the balance as their unhappy past threatens to catch up with them.

SCOTT A. GESE

BITTER IS
THE DUST

Complete and Unabridged

LINFORD
Leicester

First published in Great Britain in 2016 by
Robert Hale
An imprint of The Crowood Press
Wiltshire

First Linford Edition
published 2018
by arrangement with
The Crowood Press
Wiltshire

Copyright © 2016 by Scott A. Gese
All rights reserved

A catalogue record for this book is available
from the British Library.

ISBN 978–1–4448–3915–9

Published by
F. A. Thorpe (Publishing)
Anstey, Leicestershire

Set by Words & Graphics Ltd.
Anstey, Leicestershire
Printed and bound in Great Britain by
T. J. International Ltd., Padstow, Cornwall

This book is printed on acid-free paper

1

Jason McKinney was a survivor. The cards were stacked against him since the day he was born, and now, in his fifteenth year, he was no longer a child; yet not quite a man. Years of hard labor had made him stronger than most kids his age and it had kept him lean. His unruly mop of flaming red hair had branded him a troublemaker from an early age. He did his best to keep the reputation in good standing by bloodying the noses of most of the boys in his school at least once, no matter what the reason. At the ripe old age of twelve he was finished with school, at least, that was what he had been told by those in charge of the operation. He was happy with that to a degree; although it had kept him away from the house and the man who hated him. Nowadays it was a full time occupation to keep out of his reach.

His mother, God rest her soul, suffered complications during his birth and had died while giving him life. His father, who was in deep distress over the loss of his young wife, decided after a respectful time of grieving that he would move from his home in Wichita, Kansas, and begin a new life further east at Fort Scott. As for his newborn son, he knew nothing of caring for an infant. So, after some serious consideration and at the insistence of his younger sister, Sarah, he left the boy with her to raise as her own.

She named the boy Jason, and from his earliest childhood, the boy's life was hard. Sarah's husband, Jim, had no desire to bond with a child that was not his flesh and blood. He paid very little attention to the boy and treated him with contempt at every turn; the resulting disdain all too often unleashed in bouts of intense physical violence. To Jim, Jason was nothing more than another mouth to feed.

Accordingly, as Jason grew older, Jim

worked him hard, from sunup to sundown. The way he saw it, the harder he worked the boy the less he had to do, which translated into more time at the local saloon. Everyone in town knew Jim was a gambler and a drunk, and quite frankly, he wasn't very good at either one. At gambling, he lost more times than he won and his drinking tended to bring out his mean side which translated into the frequent beatings he handed out to his wife and Jason. Jim, however, considered himself a gentleman, justifying his actions as he bragged to the men he drank with, saying such things as 'I've never laid a hand on that woman with a closed fist,' or 'I only smack her around when she deserves it!' And as for the boy, he often boasted, ''Strong stick for a fool's back', just like the Good Book says, the ungrateful little bastard! But only when he needs it.'

That may have been true in his own drunken mind, but certainly was not fact. Jim held back most of his pent up anger and frustrations for Jason. The boy was the one on the receiving end of Jim's closed fist. And Jason, being so young, could do little more than take it.

That was until one particular day, in the summer of his fifteenth year, when a solid hickory axe handle turned the tables on the old man once and for all. It would be the last time he ever laid a hand on Jason. The first lick to the side of Jim's head would have been enough, but with all that pent up anger finally letting loose, it took more than a few good swings before the hickory stick had repaid the old man all he was owed; and with substantial interest.

When the beating had finally ended, the old man was nothing more than a heap of broken, bloody and battered bones. And as for Jason, he was taken quite by surprise, completely stunned and utterly amazed at what he had just seen his adopted mother, Sarah, finally do.

Sarah herself was more than a bit astonished at what had just taken place.

She stood silently over her husband, but the look on her face said volumes. Once she caught her breath, she threw the stick aside and looked over at Jason. He could see it in her eyes. Something had changed. Sarah was not the same woman she was five minutes ago.

'Get the horses saddled,' she ordered coldly, 'we're leaving.'

Jason wasted little time with the horses while Sarah quickly stuffed a few essentials into their saddlebags. She strapped an old pistol to her hip and shoved their only rifle into the scabbard on her saddle. Jason, not wanting to be left totally unarmed, retrieved the axe handle from where Sarah had tossed it. His 'redeemer', as he came to call it. He shoved it into his empty scabbard and swung into the saddle.

As they left the barn, Sarah's husband was still laying in the dust where he was beaten. His breathing was shallow and forced. His bones were broken and he was bleeding from several wounds. He was not in good

5

shape. Sarah had taken out some long overdue retribution upon him, and beaten him to within an inch of Hades. As the two rode past, Jason stopped long enough to look down upon the man he'd come to hate. He twice spat on the broken body lying coiled in a fetal position, then spurred his horse into a gallop to catch up with Sarah; his horse kicked up a cloud of trail dirt that covered the broken remains.

Now at a full run, they headed toward the Bradley place, their nearest neighbor. As the horses came close to the house, Sam Bradley stepped out onto the porch to meet them.

'Good afternoon, Sarah,' his voice rising as he spotted the youth and raised his hand in greeting, 'and good afternoon to you as well, young Jason. What brings the two of you by at this time of day?' Even for a close neighbor, it was rare to see the woman and her son together.

Sarah spoke up. Her voice was calm and casual. 'Sam, you best fetch Doc

Brown. Jim is back at the house and he's been hurt bad.'

Sam was a bit perplexed. 'Well, who's with him now? Why didn't you send Jason to town while you stayed and tended to him?' he anxiously questioned.

'Because,' she replied with little hesitation, 'I'm the one who hurt him. Jason and I are leaving. Please do as I ask, go fetch the doctor and take him to the house. If Jim's dead, all I can tell you is he deserved it.'

Sarah turned her horse and headed east with Jason right on her heels. Sam hurriedly saddled up his horse and rode into town to find Doc Brown. His wife, Anna, took the buggy back to Sarah's place to check on Jim.

* * *

As Anna drove up to the McKinney place, she could see Jim out front. From the way he was slowly dragging himself toward the house, she could tell he was in a lot of pain. Bringing the buggy to an abrupt halt, she quickly jumped down and ran to his side. Jim was a mess. He was covered in a mix of dust and blood. His face was horribly swollen and a deep gash on the side his head was streaming blood. His right arm was swollen and misshapen, clearly indicating it had been broken in at least two places. He was unable to stand and quite delirious as he mumbled incoherently to himself. Anna tried her best as she struggled to help him into the house, but Jim feebly shoved her away with his one good arm. 'Don't come near me, woman,' he demanded. 'I ain't hardly ever laid a hand on you and look what you did to me, and for what, showing you and that worthless boy some discipline? Go away and leave me alone!'

Once more, Anna tried to help him toward the house, but he stumbled and fell to the ground. 'Jim, I'm not Sarah, I'm your neighbor, Anna. Now get up and let me get you into the house. Sam went to get Doc Brown, they should be here soon.'

'I don't need no doctor,' moaned Jim. 'Just get me a drink or two and I'll be just fine.'

Anna ignored the request. It took some work, but she finally got him inside and sitting at the kitchen table. She filled a basin with cool water, dampened a clean cloth and began to nurse Jim's wounds as he drifted in and out of consciousness. By the time Sam and the doctor arrived, Anna had cleaned most of the blood from his face and was working on getting the dirt out of the gash on his head.

Doc Brown began his initial exam as Anna began to tell the men about how much blood she had cleaned off of him, and to complain about how all the while she was tending to him, he kept pestering her for a drink of whiskey.

'Well, did you give him one?' asked the Doc.

'I most certainly did not,' she vehemently replied; shocked he could even suggest such a thing.

'Well why not?' he scolded. 'A good

shot of strong whiskey might do him a world of good. As near as I can figure, two of these cuts will need some stitching, and from the size of the knot on his head, he probably has a concussion. He most certainly has a broken arm and a couple of broken ribs. And from the amount of swelling I see on that leg, it might be broken as well. If nothing else, a shot or two of some strong whiskey would dull his pain considerably.

'He's certainly in no condition to be moved, so bringing him into town right now is out of the question. I'll do what I can for him here. I can set his broken arm and stitch up this cut on his head, but as far as his leg is concerned, we'll just need to keep an eye on it and see how it does. I suggest somebody stay with him for a time, until he's fit enough to be moved into town.'

'He's got no kin in these parts,' replied Sam. 'If we can haul him over to our place, we can keep an eye on him for a spell.'

'And you say that his wife and son

just rode off and left him in this condition?'

'Yes sir, that's right. Sarah said we should fetch you out here because Jim was hurt bad, and that she was the one who hurt him.'

'Well I can't hardly feature it,' Doc Brown commented. 'She ain't that big of a woman. But then again, from the rumors I've heard, maybe she did do it, and maybe he had it coming, but I guess that ain't for me to say.'

After taking stock of the situation, he relented. 'I guess if hauling him over to your place is the best we can do, then I guess that's what we'll have to do. He can't be left here alone, that's for sure. I've got some laudanum in my bag. As soon as he comes around again I'll give him some for the pain. I suggest waiting until tomorrow morning before you try to move him. You'll need to figure out what you're going to do between now and then.'

'If you can stay here until dark,' offered Sam, 'Anna and I can come

11

back to sit with him until morning.'

'That'll be fine,' replied the doc 'It'll take me that long to patch him up. Help me move him over to the bed, and I'm going to need some help setting his arm before you go.'

Jim had settled down some after he got a couple shots of whiskey in him and was a bit more cooperative. Once he got moved over to the bed, Sam and the doc got busy setting the bone in Jim's arm. The pain was more than he could bear and he soon passed out. Sam and Anna left as the doc continued to patch him up.

★　★　★

After Sarah and Jason left the Bradley place, they rode hard for the rest of the day. As the sun began to set, they found a sheltered spot a short distance from the trail where they made camp for the evening. Jason built a small fire and as they sat close, soaking up its heat, the two of them silently stared into its flickering flames. Without looking up, Jason broke the long silence. 'I often wondered why you let him beat on me so.' There was something accusatory in the words. 'I figured you didn't care about me any more than he did.' Head down, he avoided looking at the woman; and then reconsidered. 'I guess maybe I was wrong.'

Sarah turned her attention from the fire and looked over at Jason. Her eyes were soft and her voice was low. As she spoke, a tear ran down the length of her cheek. 'Jim and I never had children of our own. He didn't want any. So when your father agreed to let me take you in, I was so excited. You were the welcome distraction I needed to take my mind off a loveless marriage. But Jim was against the idea from the very beginning. I thought he would take to you over time, but he never warmed up to the idea. He viewed you as competition for my attention as well as another mouth to feed.' She inhaled deeply; a long, shuddering breath, and then resumed speaking. 'I'm sorry I let him treat you the way he did. I was afraid of him, and what he was capable of. I felt so helpless for such a long time. I took the beatings he gave me, but the burden of not stopping him whenever he went after you welled up in me until I couldn't stand it any longer.' She wiped the tears from her cheeks and returned her gaze to the fire. 'I'm so sorry, Jason. I let you down for so long. You never deserved to be treated that way.'

Jason spoke softly. 'Thanks for finally sticking up for me. You were mighty brave to go after him like you did.'

She laughed, but there was no humor in the sound. 'He was drunk,' she replied.

'That may be true, but that's when he's at his meanest. You took a big risk, and as far as I'm concerned, you redeemed yourself a hundred times over the minute you picked up that axe handle and took that very first swing.'

Sarah returned her attention to Jason. 'I think it's important that you understand that your real father is a good man, Jason. He didn't abandon you because he didn't want you. He knew he couldn't raise you on his own. The death of your mother almost destroyed him, and a new baby was more than he could handle. His dreams were crushed and he felt a powerful need to get away. It was hard for him to let you go. He acted like it didn't matter, but I'm his sister. I know him and I know he was hurting the day he rode out. I hear from him from time to time. He always asks how you're doing. He does care.'

Jason's head snapped up, the surprise genuine. 'You hear from him? Where is he?'

'He's not that far away. In fact, he's still in Kansas, Fort Scott to be exact. That's where we're heading.' She was quiet for a time, and it was clear that there was going to be no more talk of her brother. 'It's been a long day, Jason,' she sighed, 'and I'm tired. I need to get some sleep and I suggest you do the same. We'll need to get an early start in the morning. No telling who might be after us.'

Unsettled, but knowing there would be no more talk, Jason threw more wood on the fire, and they both turned in for the night.

★ ★ ★

The following morning Sarah and Jason were up before the sun. The fire was re-kindled and after a hasty breakfast, they were back on the trail. Sarah figured Fort Scott was a four, maybe three-day ride if they pushed it, and that's exactly what she planned to do. Nothing would stop her from reaching her brother. Nothing would get in her way.

It was late morning on the second day. They were making good time along an old wagon trail when they first noticed the two riders approaching fast from the opposite direction. Sarah was not in a trusting mood and was wary of the two men from the time she first saw them.

'Be on your guard, Jason,' she warned before they had gotten close.

As the men reached Sarah and Jason, they slowed and came up alongside them. It was obvious they were trail-hardened men, unshaven and dirty. Their clothes were unwashed, worn and faded. One had a large scar that ran across his right cheek and disappeared somewhere behind his ear. From their stench, it was clear neither one of them had taken a bath in recent memory.

The scar-faced one spoke up. His voice was gruff and carried an unpleasant tone. 'Well, well, what have we here? A pretty young woman and a baby boy? This is mighty rough country for a couple like you to be wandering about by yourselves, don't you think? There's no telling what sort of unsavory characters you might run into out here in the middle of nowhere.'

'We're doing just fine on our own,' replied Sarah, refusing to be intimidated. She met his gaze head on. 'Do you mind if we pass?'

'Do I mind if you pass? Why, hell no I don't mind if you pass,' replied Scarface. His voice softened as he continued. 'If'n you're willing to pay the toll, that is.'

Sarah could easily see where the conversation was heading, so without giving it a second thought, she went for the gun on her hip. But Scarface had taken note of the weapon she carried and was much quicker on the draw.

As he held his gun on Sarah he remarked to his partner, 'Harper, you cover the boy. I think I'll take hold of the little woman for a bit, and extract my toll, if you know what I mean.'

'Are you sure we got time for this?' questioned Harper.

Scarface snapped back. 'We got time if'n I say we got time.' He smiled a dastardly smile toward Sarah. His half-rotted teeth only accented the repulsiveness of the situation as he stepped down from his horse and moved toward her. It was at that moment, while Harper was distracted by the sight he was hoping to witness, that Jason, in one smooth and swift motion, pulled the axe handle from his scabbard, and swung the hickory stick at Harper's face. But his aim was too low and instead of catching the man across the face as he had hoped, the stick caught him square in the throat crushing his windpipe. Harper rolled off his horse and fell to the ground clutching his throat as he gasped for air and writhed in pain. As Scarface turned toward the commotion, Sarah kicked her horse straight at him. Pulling the pistol from its holster she fired off one shot, and as pure luck would have it, she hit the scoundrel square in the left eye. He fell back and dropped to the ground with a thud as only a dead man could do.

Harper eventually quit his convulsing and lay still. Both men were now dead. Having never actually killed someone, Sarah was visibly shaken. Jason moved in close to console her. 'Are you all right?' When he saw that his words had no effect, he tried again. 'You did what you had to do. It was self defense.'

They both looked down at the bodies as they lay on the ground. 'What do you think we should do with them?' questioned Jason.

'For their mother's sake, I expect we should give them a decent burial,' replied Sarah.

Jason, not wanting to waste any time on the men, was slow to agree; but he relented. 'I expect you're right. We should bury them, but for no other reason than to hide the bodies; and the quicker the better.'

So with a hint of resignation, he dismounted and dragged the two bodies to the side of the trail where they began to cover the men over with rocks.

It was hot work, and decent sized boulders were hard to find. As they were hunting for more rocks to finish the job, two more riders came into view.

'Damn, just what we need,' stated Jason as he turned to Sarah with a concerned look on his face.

'Don't worry, let me do the talking,' cautioned Sarah as she quickly grabbed the rifle from its scabbard.

As the men came close, it was plain to see the badges that both men were wearing. One of them was a sheriff, and the other, his deputy. Nobody said a word as the lawmen looked over the situation. It was easy for them to determine what was taking place, as the dead men were only half covered.

'And what have we here?' asked the sheriff.

Sarah retorted with a swift response. 'It was self defense. These men stopped us and at gunpoint they tried to take advantage of the fact that I'm a woman. It was their last mistake.'

'So I see,' replied the sheriff. 'Do you know who these men are?'

'Scum,' interjected Jason.

'You got that right, young man.' He dismounted and uncovered the heads of the two men to get a closer look. As he examined the scar-faced one, he remarked

21

with a bit of surprise. 'You shot him in the eye.' He then turned his attention to his deputy. 'This here is Riley all right, and the other is surely Harper.' Then back to Sarah. 'These men are wanted outlaws. We've been hot on their trail most of the day. They robbed the bank back in Fall River this morning. These men were dangerous and I have to say, you two were extremely lucky things worked out the way they did.'

The sheriff walked over to the men's horses and looked through the saddlebags. From one he pulled a canvas sack with the words *Bank of Fall River, Kansas* plainly written on it. He opened it and pulled out a stack of cash of which he quickly gave an account.

'It's all here,' he remarked. 'There's a reward for these two. One hundred dollars each. I'd say you earned it.' He then counted out two hundred dollars and handed it to Sarah. 'You best be on your way, we'll take the bodies back to town for you.'

Sarah took the money and slipped it

deep into the front pocket of her pants.

After she and Jason had rode away, the deputy turned to the sheriff, the right-hand corner of his mouth quirked up in a wry smile. 'I thought there was a two hundred dollar bounty on each of these men?'

'Don't worry about it, Carson. You'll get your cut as soon as I take care of the paperwork. Get down off that horse and give me a hand. We'll load these two *hombres* up and head back to town.'

*   *   *

Jason and Sarah rode on in silence, each deep into their own thoughts. After several hours of steady riding they came upon a small creek and followed it off the trail until they came to a grove of cottonwood trees shading a small patch of grass. Sarah jumped from her horse and dropped to her knees along the bank of the creek. She repeatedly splashed its cool water onto her face as if trying to wash away the memories of the past couple of days. The water hid her tears as they streamed down her cheeks. 'What has happened to me?' she cried out, sobbing. She wrapped herself in a tight self-hug and began to rock back and forth.

'You finally came to your senses and started defending yourself,' came the voice from behind her.

She quickly turned to see Jason standing close by. 'I didn't know you were there.'

'It's all right,' he replied. 'A lot has happened in the past two days, but I know we're going to be all right; that is, as long as we keep moving.'

'But don't you understand,' cried Sarah. 'Yesterday, I beat my husband half to death, and today I killed a man.'

Jason stooped down next to Sarah and spoke to her with calm reproof. 'No, yesterday you saved the both of us from a no-good, abusive, drunk. And today you saved us from a lot worse, and you know it. We both know what they were going to do to you and there was no way in hell I was going to let that happen. Neither one of us was expecting to kill someone; and if things had gone south, we'd both be dead. It just happened.

'And to top it all off, we ended up with two hundred dollars. That sheriff didn't have to tell us there was a reward on those two men. He could have let us ride off and we wouldn't have been the wiser. Maybe he felt bad for us, I don't know. What I do know is that this is more money than either one of us has ever seen in our entire lives. So the best thing we can do now is to put this behind us and keep moving. We'll give the horses a short rest and then we go.'

Sarah stood up and kissed him on the forehead. 'Jason, you've grown up on me. You're absolutely right, but that doesn't change the fact that we took a human life . . . two of them, and as long as I live, I'll never feel good about that.'

She felt him tense beneath her fingers and decided to drop the subject. 'When we leave here we should go into town and pick up a few supplies. At the pace we're going, I figure we still have more than a two-day ride, and we're about out of food. We should steer clear of the sheriff even though he did right by us this morning. I don't know what it is; there was something about him that just didn't sit well with me. Call it a woman's intuition if you like, but I just don't trust the man.'

The summer sun continued its steady arc across a cloudless blue sky. The shadows of the day were beginning to grow as the afternoon grew late. The cool grass and the shade of the cottonwood trees would have been a welcome relief from the heat of the day but they had lingered long enough already and needed to be on the move. They mounted up and continued toward the town of Fall River, wondering if the sheriff and his deputy were still behind them, or if they had been passed without notice.

They rode for several more hours, and if they hadn't been paying attention, they would have missed the meager little town altogether. There wasn't much to it, but then, all they needed was a place to buy a few supplies. The general store was easy to find, and after hitching their horses, they went inside.

A clean-shaven middle-aged man stood behind the front counter. He was rather thin, and bald except for a band of graying hair running around the back of his head from ear to ear.

'Good afternoon, ma'am; son. What can I do for you today? Don't reckon I know you two. Are you new around here or just passing through? My name is Stewart, friends call me Gabby.'

'Well, Stewart,' replied Sarah, amused by the old man's spontaneity. 'We are just passing through and we're in need of a few supplies.'

'Yes ma'am, you just tell me what you'd like and I'll be glad to wrap it up for you. So, you're just passing through. Where might you be headin', if you don't mind my askin'?'

'Let's see,' replied Sarah, skirting the question. 'I think I'll take a small bag of those beans and a small portion of that bacon you have there, and a small sack of flour, too'

'And how about a loaf of that fresh bread I'm smelling?' inquired Jason.

'Good choice,' replied Stewart. 'My wife baked this bread just this afternoon.'

'Where might my son and I get something to eat?' inquired Sarah.

'Well . . . there is the saloon,' replied Stewart thoughtfully. 'But I don't think that's a very good place for a lady. My wife, Ellie, has just finished cooking up supper. You're welcome to eat a bite if you like. It's chicken and dumplin's, and it's mighty good eatin' if I do say so myself.'

'If you're sure you have enough, I think we'd like that,' answered Sarah. 'Now how much do I owe you?'

'That will be sixty-five cents for the supplies and since I invited you, no charge for the supper.'

Sarah reached into her front pocket and pulled out the money she had gotten from the sheriff.

'That's quite a pile of money you got there, ma'am,' exclaimed Stewart. 'I wouldn't be letting on that you got it. Around here, there are some who might try to take it from you.'

'Thank you for your concern,' replied Sarah. 'I'll keep it well hidden. Here is one dollar and you may keep the change.'

'Well, thank you, ma'am. You're very kind.' Stewart wrapped up the supplies and slipped in a second loaf of fresh bread before handing it to Sarah. 'Come along now, this way to the kitchen.' He raised his voice. 'Ellie, we have some company,' he hollered as he led the way to the back room.

Ellie walked into the kitchen where Sarah and Jason were about to be seated at the table. She was a plump woman around fortyish. A few strands of gray graced her dark brown hair and a blue gingham apron was wrapped tightly around her waist. Her pleasant smile was as bright as the noonday sun.

Stewart spoke up. 'Ellie, this here is ah . . . '

Sarah broke in. 'Sarah,' she said, extending her hand. 'And this is my son, Jason. We're just passing through and stopped to pick up a few supplies. I inquired about where we might get a bite to eat. Your husband offered his hospitality . . . and yours. I hope we're not intruding?'

'Intruding,' laughed Ellie. 'Why, we never get visitors; this is wonderful. Please, make yourselves at home. You can wash up at the basin right over here if you wish.'

Sarah took Ellie up on the offer and made her way to the basin as Jason took a seat at the table.

'So, where are the two of you traveling to?' inquired Ellie.

Stewart interrupted, 'I already asked that question Ellie, and they weren't forthcoming which is just fine by me. I believe people are entitled to their privacy.'

'Well, to be truthful,' replied Sarah as

she wiped off her wet face with a towel. 'I'm a little wary about telling folks my plans. No offense, but I think it's best if we don't say.'

Ellie dished up two plates of chicken and dumplings and set them on the table for Sarah and Jason. 'I sense the two of you may be in a bit of trouble? Would I be mistaken in thinking that?'

'Would this be like women's intuition?' asked Jason. He smiled, and risked a look at his mother.

'Why, yes, you could call it that, but even more so, I would say it was an acute eye for observing things, and seeing when they aren't just right.'

Polite conversation continued as the meal progressed. Sarah began to feel a bit more comfortable talking to Ellie and Stewart, and eventually proceeded to tell them about leaving her home and husband, but not about the beating, or the killings that took place that morning, and certainly not about where they were heading. She didn't know if her husband would eventually be

31

following them and she wasn't about to spill the beans about their destination. It felt good to talk about her troubles with another woman. Ellie, and even Stewart for that matter, were very sympathetic toward the two of them.

Soon the plates were empty and their story was told. Sarah was getting comfortable, but Jason was starting to get a little anxious about getting back on the trail.

'Ma, the horses have been tied out front for most of two hours now. We should be going before we lose any more light.'

'You're right, Jason. We've kept these good people too long from their work. We thank you for your kindness but we really do need to be moving on.'

'You're not keeping us from much,' replied Stewart. 'We don't have a whole lot to do but run this here store and as you can see, it ain't a difficult undertaking. But if you're that anxious to be heading out, we'll see you on your way.'

As they walked out the front door, they were met by the sheriff who was looking over the two horses. 'I thought I recognized these horses. I figured you two would be long past this town by now. I got me a telegram this afternoon. Seems a woman and her boy beat a man to within an inch of his life back in Wichita a couple days ago. You wouldn't happen to know anything about that now, would you?'

Ellie stepped forward. 'Now you listen here, Jonathan Brass, if she beat that man, she must have had a darn good reason to do it, so don't you be giving her a hard time or I just might let you have a good whack myself.'

Grinning, the lawman held up both hands in a gesture of surrender. 'Now just calm down, Ellie. You may be my big sister, but I have a job to do here.'

Ellie was having none of it. 'Well I suggest you go do it someplace else and leave these two alone. You need to pick your battles wisely, Jonathan, and this here ain't one of them.'

Sarah broke in. 'It's all right, Ellie. Sheriff, the man is my husband and yes, I did beat him. I'm almost sorry I didn't kill the worthless drunk. He beat me and this boy one too many times. It took me close to ten years to get up the courage to do more than just stand back and watch. My only regret is that I didn't do it sooner. If that makes me any less of a lady, then so be it. If you have nothing more to say to me, we'll be on our way.'

The sheriff locked eyes with Ellie for several seconds and then stepped aside. 'That would be a good idea. You're losing light.' A scowl and a sideways glance back at Ellie gave away the fact that Jonathan was not too happy with his big sister.

Ellie, seeing the discontent in her brother's eyes, couldn't help but dig into him just a little bit deeper. 'Just hold on there a minute, Sarah. The day is late and the sun will be down in a couple of hours. Even if you left now, you wouldn't get far before dark. If

34

Gabby has no objections, I think the two of you should stay here the night. We have an extra room, so what do you say?'

'Well that's mighty kind of you Ellie, but we really don't want to put you out and it seems the sheriff is anxious to see us leave town.'

'Don't you worry none about him. He does a darn good job for us here in Fall City, but he can be a bit over protective.' Looking toward her brother, she went on. 'I really don't think Jonathan would want to send a woman and her child out into the night. Am I right, Jonathan?'

As much as it galled him, Jonathan couldn't argue with his sister's logic. *Not that he was totally giving in.* 'On second thought, Ellie,' he replied, holding back his obvious discontent with his sister, 'I see no harm in letting them stay the night.' He shook a finger at her. 'But I'll warn you now, it's my duty to send a wire back to Wichita and let them know I've seen these two. But just to show you how high and mighty I can be, I'll tell you what. I won't send that telegram until tomorrow morning after they've left town.' Politely tipping the brim of his hat, he took his leave, making damned sure he had the last word. 'You all have a pleasant evening.'

Ellie turned to Sarah with a big grin on her face. 'See how easy that was. He acts tough, but he's a pushover if you handle him right. Now I won't take no for an answer. The two of you just turn yourselves right around and head back inside. And thank you, Gabby, for not objecting.'

'Ain't nothing to object to. I'll take the horses around back and bed 'em down for the night.'

★   ★   ★

Sheriff Brass felt uneasy about having Sarah and the boy hanging around. He hadn't said anything about them killing the two bank robbers. When he and Carson brought the bodies back into

36

town, he just let everyone believe they had killed them. He had lied on the paperwork he filled out earlier and now was hoping he wouldn't be found out. His sister Ellie was hard headed, but even if they did confide in her about what happened, she would keep her mouth shut. She liked the notoriety that having her brother as sheriff gave her.

It was late the following morning when Sheriff Brass walked through the door of the general store. Stewart was busying himself at the counter.

'I haven't seen those two ride out yet and daylight's burning.'

'Ellie's a hard headed woman, John,' Stewart shrugged. 'She ain't about to let those two ride out on their own again.'

Jonathan was toying with a bolt of fabric laying out on the counter. 'I don't believe that was our agreement. Where is she, Gabby? I need to have a talk with her about that.'

Stewart responded without looking at his brother-in-law. 'Hang on and I'll get her for you.'

Stewart went into the back room and a few seconds later Ellie came out . . . alone.

Jonathan wasted no time in calling his sister out. 'What the hell is going on here, Ellie? Gabby tells me you're holding those two back. Didn't I say I wanted them out of town at first light?'

'That was before Sarah confided in me last night about the two dead holdup men you brought in from the desert yesterday. Seems you and Carson weren't the ones who killed them after all, but you let the whole town believe you were. I'm not going to let that woman and her son ride out of here without an escort. It's too dangerous. Sarah and I went to the telegraph office earlier this morning and sent for her brother over in Fort Scott.'

The lawman threw up his hands in disgust. 'Fort Scott! That's a good two days ride from here.'

'That's right, and if you don't want people in this town to look down on you for taking credit for dragging in those two dead outlaws yesterday, I suggest you put up with them for a couple more days. They're good people, Jonathan, if you would just stop thinking of them as a threat and start seeing them for who they are, you'd realize that.'

'I ain't happy about this, Ellie,' grumbled the sheriff, perturbed that his older sister had an annoying way of forgetting just who was in charge. 'But as long as everyone keeps their mouths shut, I'll let it be.'

'No one will say a word,' Ellie promised as she turned and headed to the back room. It took all the control she could muster to hide her laughter.

⋆ ⋆ ⋆

Mac Shepard had just finished loading his wagon with a few supplies. He didn't come to town often. He pretty much kept to himself and only made the trip in when he was running low on the basic necessities. As a younger man, he had fought in the War Between the States. He was battle hardened, but even that had not prepared him for the horrific pain of the sudden loss of his young wife during the birth of his one and only son.

Letting go of the boy had been even worse.

Rubbing the sweat from his brow, he shook the grim thoughts away. He'd spent too many years living in the Hell of 'what if' and 'if only'; beating himself almost to the ground with regret and guilt, each passing year worse than the one before. At first, he had contented himself with the knowledge his sister Sarah would provide his son the tender mercies a baby needed. Later, he consoled himself with the thought that he had very little to offer the boy, at least, not yet; and life moved on, one day passing to the other like pages turning in a book.

Someone calling his name roused him from his dark musings, and he looked up to see the young boy from the Western Union jogging his way and calling his name. 'Mr Shepherd!'

Hesitating, he took the piece of paper from the boy's hand, his brow furrowing as he began to read. Almost as an afterthought, he dug in to the front pocket of his trousers, and dug out a two-cent piece and handed it off to the kid.

Two days later, just as the sun was cresting over the general store, a stranger rode into town. Sheriff Brass leaned against the hitch rail in front of his office, enjoying the warmth of the early morning sun. He busied himself with rolling a smoke while keeping a keen eye on the man heading in his direction. The newcomer pulled up in front of the sheriff and tipped his hat in a polite fashion.

'Good morning, sheriff. I'm looking for a woman named Sarah McKinney. You wouldn't happen to know where I might find her, would you?'

The sheriff finished rolling his smoke and put a match to it. He studied the stranger through a haze of fresh smoke before he answered with a question of his own. 'This wouldn't happen to be the Sarah who travels with a young red headed boy named Jason now would it?'

Suddenly wary, the man nodded his head. 'Yes, that would be her.'

Brass flicked some dead ash from his quirly. 'You must be her brother. I'm afraid I didn't catch your name?'

'My apologies. My name is Mac, Mac Shepard.'

'Well, Mac Shepard, you can find your sister right across the street at the general store.'

'Thank you, sheriff.' Mac sat still, only turning his head in the direction of the store. He sat there on his horse not saying a word and not moving one way or the other.

The sheriff took a long draw from his smoke. He watched the sun filter through the lazy blue haze as he slowly exhaled. Seeing that Mac hadn't made a move, he inquired. 'What seems to be the problem there, Mac?'

Turning back to the sheriff, he replied. 'The boy is my son. I pretty much abandoned him when he was born. His mother died during child-birth and I had no clue about taking care of a newborn child. I left him with my sister, and I left town.'

Brass heard something akin to regret in the man's voice; regret and uncertainty. 'And you haven't seen him since?'

Mac shook his head. 'No, sir. I've gotten word about him from time to time, but I felt too guilty to come back to see him.'

The sheriff took another long drag from his smoke and blew it out thoughtfully. 'You could have came back to fetch him once he got older,' he replied.

Mac Shepherd squared his shoulders, mouthing the words he had said a hundred times in his head during the long ride into town. 'No sir, I couldn't do that. Jason was the son Sarah never

43

had. I couldn't take him away from her. It wouldn't have been right.'

The lawman snorted. 'Of course not, but you're here now. So man up and go take care of business.'

Mac stepped off his horse and slowly led it across the street to the hitch rail where he tied it. Heavy-footed, he stepped up on the boardwalk and disappeared through the store's front door.

Sheriff Brass walked off down the street. He had work to do.

'How may I help you,' inquired Stewart, as Mac came through the door.

'My name is Mac Shepard. I'm looking for a woman named Sarah. I understand she's here.'

Before Stewart had a chance to reply, Sarah burst through the back room doorway and rushed into the arms of her brother. She hugged him hard and the tears began to flow.

Ellie, watching from the doorway, dried her own eyes with the edge of her apron.

Through tears of joy, Sarah and Mac

expressed their sorrows for not contacting each other more often.

After several minutes of conciliatory small talk, Mac could hold back the question no longer. 'Where is he, where's Jason?'

Sarah turned toward the back room and Ellie stepped out of the doorway. 'Jason,' she called. 'Come out here and meet your father.'

Nothing.

'Jason,' Sarah called again.

Jason slowly stepped into the doorway.

Sarah beckoned to the boy with her right hand, wiggling her fingers. 'Jason, come here. I want you to meet my brother, Mac . . . your father.'

Jason and Mac looked at each other warily. Neither one was sure of what to expect. Finally, after what seemed like an eternity, Jason spoke up. 'You son-of-a-bitch! You left me in the hands of the devil himself and you never came back to save me.'

Bewildered — visibly shocked — Mac

looked to Sarah. 'What's he talking about?'

Sarah, stunned by Jason's comment, called out. 'Jason, he doesn't know. I never told him.'

'Never told me *what?*' demanded Mac.

Jason, tears streaming down his cheeks, angrily shouted. 'That the man you left me with was a worthless gambler and drunk!! When he drank too much or he lost all his money, he would take it out on us. He would beat me and he would beat Ma too. He was the devil and I hope someday he burns in hell!'

Sarah again cried out. 'Jason, it's not Mac's fault. I never told him. *I never told him*!'

Mac, now more angry than confused, turned to Sarah. 'You let this go on for how many years and never once called out to me for help? I'll kill that son-of-a-bitch. I swear to God, I'll kill him!'

'No Mac, you won't,' Sarah admonished. 'What we need to do right now is to keep moving forward. We need to go to your place where we can be safe, and sort things out. Killing him would be the wrong thing to do.'

'I'm all for killing him,' scoffed Jason, not caring who heard. 'Hell, I'd like nothin' more than to find out Dull Knife and his band of Cheyennes . . . '

Appalled by her son's outburst, Sarah cut him off. 'Didn't you hear what I just said? No! At some point he'll come looking for us. You can be sure of that, and when he does, I want to be someplace safe.'

Ellie broke in. 'Sarah, if that man comes into this town, take my word for it. I'll personally make sure he goes no further.'

Mac spoke up. 'Jason, I'm upset that Sarah never told me about how it was with the two of you. Believe me, if I had known, I would have put an end to it a long time ago. I'm sorry I left you. My wife, your mother, died giving you birth. I couldn't handle it and I couldn't handle a newborn baby. I ran.

I know that was a coward thing to do, and for that I'm truly sorry. I know I may never be able to make it up to you, but please give me the chance.'

Stewart, who had been quietly observing the whole scene, and having a good idea where the situation was heading, took it upon himself to speak up. 'Jason, why don't you and I go out and saddle up the horses.'

He gave Mac a friendly wink as he ushered Jason out the back door and into the barn where the horses were stalled. Jason was still in a foul mood as he backed up against the stall gate in a huff. 'Did you hear him! He admitted it! He ran. He dropped me like a hot rock and ran off.' That fact his father had apologized mattered not one mote.

Reaching out, Stewart laid a gentle hand on the boy's shoulder. 'Listen, Jason, you don't really know me and you can take what I'm about to say with a grain of salt if you like, but please do the respectful thing and stay here while I talk. I'm a pretty simple man. I'm not a deep thinker like some, but I have had ample opportunity in my life to observe people. I know I'm good at reading them and I know when someone's hurting deep inside. I seen it in you and Sarah the first day the two of you walked into my store, and believe it or not, I see it in your father right now.'

'*He's* not my father,' argued Jason vehemently.

Stewart shook his head. 'But that's where you're wrong. He is your father whether you want to claim him or not, and believe me, he's hurting right now just as you are. I'm sure at the time he left, he thought he was doing the right thing. Think about how he must have felt. His wife, your mother, had just died. He knew he couldn't take care of you. He thought he was leaving you in capable hands. Why heck, nobody can read the future. He did what he thought was best for you. I'm sure it was a hard decision for him, don't you think? Right or wrong, you have to give the man credit for making such a hard decision.

He's definitely mad at Sarah for not confiding in him about what was happening to the two of you, and I'm sure he feels guilty about it. After all, he did apologize and he did ask for another chance to make it right. You really need to consider your next move here, Jason. You have the opportunity to have a new beginning with a real father. One who I'm sure will care for you.

'You have a decision to make, boy.' He gave the youngster a little shake. 'I'll saddle the horses while you think about what it is you're going to do next.'

Stewart pulled a blanket off the rail and began to saddle one of the horses. Jason stayed where he was for another minute before he slowly began to walk back to the house. Stewart stopped and watched him go and hoped he had talked some sense into the boy.

Jason stepped back into the house. Ellie was out front waiting on a customer. Sarah and Mac sat at the kitchen table, talking. Mac rose up from his chair and faced Jason as the boy walked into the room; watching as his son stopped cold in his tracks. Silently, they faced each other, until Jason walked up to Mac and offered his hand. 'My name is Jason.'

Relieved, Mac accepted the hand. 'My name is Mac.'

'It'll be good to get to know you, Mac,' Jason said, his tone subdued. 'Now let's get moving.'

'*It's a start*,' thought Mac. '*It's a start*.'

By the time Mac, Sarah and Jason were out the front door, Stewart had the horses saddled and waiting. Sheriff Brass stood nearby as they said their good-by's and mounted up. He was happy to see them go and tipped his hat to Sarah as she rode past. Jason, who was taking up the rear stopped next to the sheriff and leaned in. 'I hear the reward for those two men who robbed the bank was two hundred each. You owe me two hundred dollars.'

Sheriff Brass was quick to react as he reached up and grabbed Jason by the shirt jerking him off his horse and down into the dirt. He planted his boot on the boy's chest and pulled his revolver from its holster. Thinking better of the move, he reholstered his gun, but with his boot still firmly planted he leaned in close and said his piece. 'Why you little shit. If you were more than a little red headed runt, I'd work you over good. You're lucky you got what you did. If you want to push the matter it'll be my pleasure and your big mistake. I suggest you crawl back on that horse and catch up with your mama . . . and don't look back.'

By this time, Mac and Sarah had turned back. 'Is there a problem here, sheriff?' asked Mac.

'I don't believe so. Is there, Jason?'

Jason got up out of the dirt and brushed himself off. 'Not at the moment,' he replied as he climbed back onto his horse.

The three of them continued down the street, Mac and Sarah in the lead deep in conversation. Jason turned and looked back at the sheriff with disdain, and then, certain Sarah and Mac were not watching — nor giving a damn at what the sheriff had threatened — raised his arm in a one-fingered salute. Laughing, he spun his horse around and spurred it into a lope, intent on catching up with his companions.

Later in the day as he rode alongside Sarah, she asked, 'Back in town, what was that all about with you and the sheriff?'

'Nothing, nothing at all.'

'It looked to be a little more than nothing to me,' Sarah ventured.

Eyes straight ahead, Jason shrugged it off. 'Don't worry about it. The sheriff and I just don't see eye to eye on a certain thing.'

'And what thing is that?' Sarah persisted.

'Like I said, don't worry about it. It was nothing.'

2

Benjamin Dunn

Under the cloak of darkness, Benjamin Dunn quickly stepped out the back door of his parents' house. The gas lamp held high by his father revealed the family's fastest horse as it stood saddled and waiting. A kiss on his mother's cheek and a hurried handshake to his father, marked the end of a promising career and the beginning of a new adventure.

Not exactly the plan he had mapped out for himself, but current circumstances were forcing him to quickly make drastic decisions. There was no time to waste. His very life was in danger, so it was either flee until the situation calmed and was forgotten, or hang at the hands of a group of narrow-minded vigilantes who were at this very moment on their way to his parents' house to seize him.

His uncle, on his mother's side, lived out west. The hastily laid plan was for him to head there until word arrived telling him it was safe to return home. The mob would surely look for him around town, but none would suspect that a wealthy professional from Virginia would ever consider hiding out in the unrefined wilds of Kansas.

'Well then, I'm off,' he stated as he stepped up into the saddle.

'I've packed your bags with a few provisions, but you'll need to get supplies once you're clear of danger. God speed to you, my son. Get word to your mother and I when you arrive and we'll keep you informed on the situation here. Now go before it's too late!'

The dim light of the gas lamp quickly gave way to the darkness as Benjamin Dunn disappeared into the night.

There was little time for tears and good-by waves as more pressing business was in need of their attention. Mr and Mrs. Dunn went back into the house to prepare for the eventual arrival of the angry mob that was intent on lynching their son.

Even though he wasn't a politician himself, Nathanial J. Dunn was influential in Virginia politics. His wealth came from real estate speculation. Richmond was the heart of the Confederacy, and during the war it was considered the new capital of the South. Nathaniel had the uncanny ability to foresee upcoming events almost before they unfolded and he was quick to take advantage of situations long before others were even aware of their existence. It's this ability that made him a wealthy man. And with his money directed toward the right causes, and people of power, it bought him the influence he needed to continue his upward movement in both Richmond, and Virginia society.

Unfortunately, his son had set his own course. As a respected physician and outspoken advocate for the Negro cause, he became a liability to some and a danger to others.

The mob that would soon reach Nathanial's door had been bought and paid for by men of means who were intent on stifling their son's views once and for all. Fortunately, Nathanial knew how to deal with these types. The war had left many in the area poor and destitute, and such were these men. The cause was of less concern to them as the money they were paid to carry out the lynching. When they arrived, he would allow them access to the house to conduct their search. Once they were satisfied that Benjamin was not there, he would feed them a hearty meal, then pay them off and send them on their way. They would leave satisfied, in more ways than one. And that would be the end of the situation. For the time being, it would relieve the symptoms, but not the cause. To do that, he would need to resort to other, more sophisticated and political methods, if he ever expected to see his son back in Richmond again.

* ★ ★

Benjamin Dunn traveled swiftly through the night and for most of the following day before he afforded himself and his horse the luxury of slowing down the pace. He and his mount were both exhausted and needed to find a secure place to rest. He eventually found a small grassy meadow along a narrow creek where he could get a few hours sleep as well as water and feed his horse.

Once settled, he rummaged through the hastily packed bag to see what he might find to eat. A few dry biscuits and some cheese was the extent of the food. There was also a change of clothes, and to his surprise, several large bundles of cash.

Along with his horse and saddle, this was the sum total of what he now owned. A far cry from the luxuries he enjoyed less than twenty-four hours ago. He smiled as he counted out the cash. He may not have agreed with his father on the politics of the day, but they both understood the power of money, and the amount Ben carried with him would be more than sufficient to ease his journey to Kansas. After a sufficient rest, he was back on the trail and heading for Lynchburg.

Upon reaching the town of Lynchburg, he was able to secure train passage for himself and his horse all the way to Bristol, Tennessee, where he found a stable for his horse and himself a warm bed for the evening. From Bristol, by way of both track and trail, Benjamin easily made his way to the frontier town of Fort Scott, Kansas where his uncle owned a large cattle ranch not too far from town.

Even though the journey to Fort Scott had been smooth, the destination didn't come soon enough. He was feeling a bit ragged and in need of a bath and shave. A clean set of clothes would be a good idea as well, before heading out to his uncle's ranch.

Fort Scott was the home of almost four thousand, a small town compared to Richmond, so finding what he needed was a relatively easy task. He stabled his horse and quickly located a bath and a barber. Once he cleaned himself up he found a nearby store where he could purchase a new set of clothes. Being out west in the 'Wild Frontier', he felt he needed to dress more 'Western'. Even though he had done away with his tie days earlier, his dirty white shirt and slacks had to go. Recalling pictures from books he had read as a child, about cowboys and wild Indians, he picked out what he thought were appropriate clothes for a man of prominence out west. After making his purchase, he found a nice hotel where he secured a room for the evening.

The following morning he put on his new clothes, which included a white shirt with matching yellow plaid jacket and pants, complete with suspenders. A set of boots and a hat rounded out the new outfit. After admiring his new suit from in a mirror at the top of the stairs, he headed down to the dining area for a late breakfast. As he sat at one of the empty tables, he was approached by a waiter.

'You have 'remarkable' taste in clothing,' he commented.

'Well, thank you,' Ben replied. 'I'm new around these parts and I thought this would be appropriate attire for a man of stature, trying to fit in.'

'Ahh . . . good luck to you sir,' came the hesitant reply.

After a hearty breakfast he asked the waiter if he knew how to get to the XO ranch. The waiter did know the way, but he thought he'd have some fun with the oddly dressed 'man of stature' and suggested he head two blocks down the street to the Hoof and Horn saloon where the bartender would most likely be able to give him directions. Ben thanked the waiter for his hospitality, and as he left, he thought he heard the waiter laughing, but didn't pay much attention other than to think he had just missed something rather hilarious.

The waiter's directions were good,

and Ben soon found the Hoof and Horn saloon right where he said it would be. From the outside, it didn't look like a very high-class establishment, but since it was recommended by his waiter, who had seemed a decent sort, he timidly pushed his way through the batwings and walked up to the bar. A few young and boisterous cowboys were enjoying a drink after gathering morning supplies, and as Benjamin walked across the room a couple of the boys began to point and snicker. One of the men began to outright laugh.

'Keep yer mouth shut, Wes,' the bartender shouted to the boys at the table before turning his attention on the new arrival. 'Those are some mighty fine lookin' boots you've got there, mister. I love the way you tuck those fine checkered pants you're wearin' down inside of 'em.'

More laughter from several of the boys caused the bartender to give them the evil eye, which shut them up directly.

'And that ten-gallon hat you got on goes real well with the rest of yer outfit, I might add,' the bartender continued, struggling to keep a straight face as he kept on wiping the same glass. 'My guess is you're new in town.'

'I'm no fool,' replied Ben, his eyes narrowing as he pulled himself erect. 'I can tell when I'm being made fun of.'

'No harm intended, mister, I'm just funnin' with you a bit. No harm meant by it at all. If you don't mind my sayin', that shirt you got on might be OK, but I would seriously consider losing that jacket and those fancy pants you got on.' He ended his advice with a broad smile. 'My name is Charley, Charley O'Donnell. My friends call me Ira. What can I do for you?'

'I was wondering if you might be able to direct me to the XO ranch?'

'The XO, Now that all depends. Are you a carpetbagger?'

'No, sir, Mr O'Donnell, I'm looking for a job.'

'A job? Well, I don't know if they're

hiring, but as luck would have it, if Wes here can shut his snickering mouth and pick himself up off the floor for a minute, he may be able to help you out. He works for the XO and was just about to head back that way. He'd be glad to take you. Isn't that right, Wes?'

'Why sure,' replied Wes, with a wide smile on his face. 'I'd be glad to show him the way out to the XO.' Looking toward Ben, he asked, 'Do you have a horse?'

'Why yes, I do. He's stabled just a few blocks from here.'

'Then go get it and meet me back here in five minutes, or you'll have to find another way out to the XO.'

As Ben left to get his horse he remarked that he would need to purchase another pair of pants and stop by the hotel to change and pick up his belongings.

'No time for that,' replied Wes. 'Grab up your gear and fetch your horse. You've got five minutes.'

As Ben left the saloon, Ira couldn't

help but chuckle. 'Can you believe this guy! What kind of a job do you think he's expecting to get? I wonder if he even knows what a cow is. And what's the big idea telling him he doesn't have time to get new trousers? He has plenty of time.'

'No, sir,' replied Wes. 'If I'm taking him back to the XO, he's going there dressed just the way he is, ten-gallon hat and all.' He laughed.

Ben hurried back to the hotel, grabbed his bag and settled his bill, and then high tailed it over to the livery where he paid up, saddled up and headed out the door. It took more than five minutes, but Wes was patiently waiting for him in front of the Hoof and Horn with a wagon full of supplies, when he arrived.

'You want me up in the wagon with you?' asked Ben.

'No sir,' replied Wes. 'You follow along behind. The XO is only a two hour ride from here. We'll be there long before dark.'

Ben enjoyed the ride as the road wove through tall prairie grass and plenty of grazing cattle. In what seemed like no time at all, they came to a turn off that lead to the main house of the XO ranch. As they arrived, several of the men were washing up for supper. Wes stood up on the wagon and pointed at Ben. 'Gather 'round, boys, take a look at what followed me home. Do you think the boss will let me keep him?'

The men all laughed as one replied, 'Looks like one of them exotic pets.' Another called out, 'Looks like he came straight off the cover of one of them dime novels.'

Another roar of laughter from the men ensued.

About that time, Miles Hanley, the owner of the XO, stepped out the front door. 'What's all the commotion out here?'

'Wes brought home a stray,' replied one of the men.

More laughter.

'I see that,' replied Miles. 'What's your name son and what can I do for you?'

'My name is Ben Dunn and I'm looking for a job.'

'Ben Dunn you say. And where are you from Mr Dunn?'

'I'm from Virginia, Richmond to be exact.'

The laughter of the men suddenly became mute.

'That's Confederate territory, my men and I fought for the Union.'

'I'm from Richmond, sir. But that doesn't mean I subscribed to the confederate way of thinking. I kept my mouth shut during the war and never fired a shot. I only recently spoke up against southern politics. Unfortunately, I paid the price for it.'

'How so?'

Ben leaned forth slightly, his voice lowering as he stroked the animal's neck. 'May we talk in private, sir?'

'Ben Dunn you say. Sure, step down off that horse and come inside, let's do some talking. One of you men take care of his horse. The rest of you unload that wagon and then get yourselves some grub. Ben, that outfit you're wearing looks like hell.'

'I realize that,' he replied, as he stepped off his horse and grabbed his bag.

Miles and Ben walked into the house and closed the door.

'Can you feature that?' remarked Wes. 'I didn't think that slicker would make it off his horse, let alone into the house. Now I've seen it all.'

'Great hat!' came the sarcastic remark by one of the men as they commenced to unload the wagon. 'With dandies like that coming out of Richmond, it's no wonder we won the war.'

The two men entered the front room and Miles offered Ben a seat. 'Ben Dunn, from Richmond you say. Well I'll be damned. Tell me Ben, what's your mother's name?'

'You should know that. It's Louise, Louise Hanley-Dunn, originally from

Kentucky. She married into money and moved to Richmond.'

'Yes sir, that's my sis. And you're her son. Last I heard you were on your way to becoming a doctor, right?'

'It's a long story and someday I'll fill you in on all the details. Right now all I can say is that I had to leave town in a hurry, as there was a lynch mob literally at the door looking to stretch my neck for no good reason.'

'Is my sister safe?'

'Yes, she and my father should be fine. As you know, he's very influential in Richmond. No harm will come to either of them.'

The rancher's eyes narrowed as he appraised his new discovered nephew. 'And what you did is not illegal? I don't have to worry about the law showing up at my door, do I?'

Ben shook his head. 'No sir. In fact, I hope to get back to Richmond at some point, when things calm down. There's still a lot of hard feelings with the war so recent and all.'

'You can say that again, Kansas was a mixed bag. We see it around here quite often. You're welcome to stay on at the XO for as long as you need. I'm willing to pay you a decent wage, but you need to hold up your end.'

'I appreciate that, Miles.' Ben opened up his bag and pulled out the stacks of cash. 'My parents didn't send me out unprepared. You're welcome to pay my wage and any other expenses you may incur on my account, from this. Do you have a safe place to keep it until I leave?'

Miles laughed. 'Isn't that just like my sis. I'll hold on to this for you and if I get a decent day's work from you, I'll give you a decent day's wage from my own pocket. It's only fair. In the mean time, you'll work, eat and sleep with the rest of the men. I won't say anything more than I hired you. I'll let you work out the details of the story you'll tell the men. Let me get you a decent pair of pants and a different hat. That shirt will do for now.'

After Ben had changed his clothes and slipped some of the money he had given Miles, into his pocket, the two of them went out to the bunkhouse to meet the rest of the hands.

The men had finished eating and were relaxing around the table as they played a hand of poker for toothpicks.

'I see you boys are playing by my rules, no poker for money here at the ranch. I appreciate that. Boys, I'd like you to meet the new hand. This here is Ben Dunn.' Pointing to each man in turn he named them off. 'Ben, this here is Smiley, this is Little Walt, this here is Zane and this, which you've already met, is Wes. Wes, I heard you ask earlier if you could keep Ben. Well, the answer is yes, he's your responsibility. I expect you'll teach him right.'

Wes's face blanched. He immediately sensed he was being punished for his earlier shenanigans, but wasn't sure why. 'I was only kidding, Miles,' he muttered.

'Well, I'm not. Maybe you should be

more careful about what you ask for now, shouldn't you?'

The rest of the men were getting a good laugh at Wes's expense as Miles went back up to the house.

'Great, OK Ben, tell us how a dandy from Richmond managed to get himself hired on at the XO, and get the boss to give you a pair of his pants and a hat to boot.'

Ben did his best to convince the men he had qualifications, but they were having no part of it.

* * *

The next morning, Zane, the XO's foreman, sent Wes and Ben out to ride the eastern fence line and repair several breaches that were known to exist as well as look for others. On their ride out, Wes did his best to strike up a conversation.

'So, Ben, have you ever repaired fence before?'

'No, but I can't imagine it would be too hard.'

'Oh, you can't, can you. Tell me, have you done any ranch work at all? My guess is no. I mean, you don't look like you've spent much time in the sun and you don't have one callus on your hands. My God man, you don't even carry a gun. So tell me again, what have you done all your life?'

Ben shrugged, not wanting to give anything away he couldn't back up. 'It's like I told you last night, I've worked with horses.'

'Yes, that's what you told us last night, but that's mighty vague, don't you think? Did you break 'em, shoe 'em, doctor 'em . . . What?'

'All of it,' replied Ben.

'All of it, you say. Well now, that's mighty interesting, Ben, mighty interesting. I do know this much. You don't dress like a ranch hand, your horse ain't no workin' horse, and that saddle? I've never seen a saddle quite like that before. You ain't foolin' none of the men at the XO and you certainly ain't foolin' me. We know you haven't done a single day of ranch work in your entire life, and I don't know what the hell you told the boss to get him to hire you. The way I figure it, you two are hiding something from the rest of us and my guess is today is day one of your ranching experience. So why don't we see what you're worth.'

Ben did his best to change the subject. 'My saddle? It's a riding saddle.'

Ben's reluctance to respond to Wes's concerns aggravated him all the more. 'Well that's just great, Ben, 'cuz Lord knows, you'll be doing a lot of that. Thing is, you'll also be doing a lot of working. What you really need is a working saddle. Maybe you can get the boss to give you one of them too.'

Ben was no fool. He knew sarcasm when he heard it, and he knew he had a long way to go to prove himself to Wes, and the rest of the men as well.

Wes worked Ben hard for most of the week. By the time Friday evening came around, Ben thought he was actually getting the hang of setting posts and stretching wire. He was wrong about it not being too hard though. He had never worked so hard in all his life and was secretly hoping his stay at the XO would be short.

Friday was payday and the tradition with the men at the XO was to head into town that night and make their way back to the ranch before the weekend was over.

'We're heading into town, care to come with us, Ben?' asked Zane.

'Thanks for the invitation, but I'm sore and I'm beat. I think I'll pass. You all have a good time and drink a beer for me. I'm going down early tonight.'

'Suit yourself. We'll be back in the morning . . . maybe.'

'I need to take care of some business in town tomorrow morning. Maybe I'll meet up with you and the boys and we can ride back together.'

'We'll be at the Hoof and Horn. Think you can find it?'

'I've been there once before, so that

shouldn't be a problem.'

Zane shut the door and Ben collapsed on his bunk.

★ ★ ★

The next morning Ben was up early. He took care of a few small chores before heading into town. He did have some pressing business to take care of and was anxious to get it done before the XO men headed back to the ranch. On the ride in, he couldn't help but think about how he enjoyed the quiet openness of the prairie, the smell of tall grass and even the cattle. It was nothing like the noisy bustle of Richmond, which he was beginning to see in a whole different light.

Once in town, his first stop was the livery where he had kept his horse the previous week. As he entered, he noticed the horses of the XO men were still there. An older man in the loft, which only covered over the stalls, was pitching hay. He poked his head over the edge and called down. 'What can I do for you?'

'I'm looking to board my horse, and I was wondering if you happen to have any new saddles?'

'Hang on, I'll be right down.'

Ben talked with the man and found out he didn't have any new saddles, but did have a couple of good used saddles for sale. After a bit of negotiating, he traded off his and a few dollars more for a nice working saddle. He also found out what the men would owe for boarding their horses and paid their bill in advance. After taking care of business, he went back to the same store where he had bought his clothes earlier and purchased a new pair of pants, shirt and hat. The storekeeper let him use the back room to change into his new clothes. From there, he walked over to the postmaster's to see if any messages had arrived for him. He knew it hadn't been near long enough, but he was anxious to get some news of the situation back home. As he had thought, there was nothing for him. That was the last of the errands he needed to run, so he headed over to the Hoof and Horn to see if any of the XO men were there. They were.

Ben pushed his way through the batwings and up to the bar. Ira, the bartender had to take a second look before he realized who it was.

'Well, if it isn't mister fancy pants. Looks like somebody wised you up to the dress code around here?'

'It's been one heck of a week,' replied Ben. 'I've been wised up to more than a few things around here.' Looking over the room, He spotted Wes and the rest of the men sitting at one of the tables. 'What, no laughing,' he stated.

'No laughing this time,' replied Wes.

'We were just about to head out,' stated Zane. 'Are you ready to go?'

'I'd like to buy you all a drink first, unless you're in a hurry?'

'When a fella' offers to buy a man a drink, the only polite thing to do is to oblige him,' stated Little Walt.

'Well in that case, Ira, a round for me and my friends.'

This was the first time all week, Ben actually felt like he was making some headway with the boys. After they finished their drinks, they all headed down to the livery. As they went to settle up the bill they were told it had already been taken care of.

'Taken care of? By who?'

'Why this gent here,' replied the stableman as he pointed out Ben.

'It was the least I could do for you all after putting up with me this week. I know it hasn't been easy.'

They all thanked Ben for being so generous, and as they began to saddle up their horses, Little Walt and Smiley noticed Ben had himself a new saddle and began to talk amongst themselves.

'What are you two mumbling about over there,' asked Zane.

Little Walt spoke up. 'Smiley and me was just wonderin' what the heck is going on around here.'

'What do you mean?' asked Zane.

'I mean Ben Dunn, from Richmond, Virginia no less, comes ridin' onto the XO last week all gussied up like a dime store cowboy. He don't know beans about ranching, or cattle. He git's himself invited into the bosses' house where he git's himself a pair of pants and a hat from the boss himself, and to top it all off, he gits himself hired on regular like, and we gits to babysit him. Now, after only a week on the payroll, he buys himself new clothes and a new saddle, he buys us drinks and pays our bill.'

'So, what's your point, Walt?' asked Zane.

'My point is . . . where's he gittin' all the money? Is he gittin' paid more 'an us, or what?'

'I really don't think that's any of your business,' replied Zane.

'Well I think it is my business. And I wanna' know what the heck mister Ben Dunn has to say about it.'

'I think it's none of your business,' Ben replied.

'None of my business, well we'll see about that. Maybe I'll just make it my business.'

Little Walt advanced toward Ben with clenched fists and the look of fire in his eyes, but Zane stepped in front of him and cut him off. 'Like the man said, it's none of your business. Now fork that horse and ride out.'

Little Walt was peeved, but kept his mouth shut as he went back to saddling his horse. He never got the answer he was looking for, but the question did get the rest of the men to thinking. As they mounted up and headed out of the livery, they were met by two riders just coming in. They were a couple of rough looking, trail worn characters and both in need of a shave and a bath. One of the men spit a stream of tobacco juice into the dirt and in a low, gravely sort of voice, asked the boys, 'Are ye Yanks', or Rebs'?'

Zane, knowing full well that there were men around who still hadn't accepted the defeat of the South, kept his mouth shut. But Little Walt, being proud to have served in the Union spouted off, 'Yanks, and proud of it.'

'Wrong answer,' shouted the stranger as he and his partner drew their pistols and began to fire.

Little Walt was hit square in the chest. Smiley, Wes and Zane pulled their guns and returned fire, but not before Wes was hit in the shoulder. Zane and Smiley shot straight and the two men went down. One last dying shot from one of the men hit Smiley's horse. It dropped to the ground and Smiley rolled off into the dirt, but was quickly on his feet, shouting in disbelief, 'He shot my horse. That no good jasper shot my horse.' Suddenly realizing Little Walt had been shot, he continued, 'and Walt too.'

Ben jumped from his horse and was at little Walt's side in less than a heartbeat. Walt was still breathing, but losing blood from the hole in his chest.

'Somebody get the doc,' shouted Smiley.

'Can't do that,' answered the stable-man. 'Doc Evans went out to the Dunkin place early this morning to deliver a baby. No telling when he'll be back.'

Ben began to tear open Walt's shirt to get a better look at the wound. 'No time to wait for the doctor, this man needs attention now. Lead the way to his office, we'll take him there.'

'Didn't you just hear the man? The doc is out of town. What the hell are you talking about, Ben?' asked Zane.

'Look,' Ben started, gesturing, 'he's been shot in the chest. See how hard he's breathing and how the blood flowing from the wound has small bubbles around it? My guess is one of his lungs has collapsed. He needs attention now, Zane. We can't wait for Doc Evans. I'll take care of him myself.'

'I'm lost here, Ben. What the hell are you talking about?'

'Zane, I'm a doctor, and a damn good one I might add. I'll explain it all to you later, but right now we need to get Walt to the doc's place where I can get at this wound.'

Zane, not quite believing what Ben had just told him, hesitated for a second as he decided whether or not to place the life of Little Walt in this man's hands. But his concern was so deep for Little Walt, plus the fact that he really didn't have much of a choice, he took him at his word. 'You heard the man. Let's get him to the doc's place. Somebody lead the way.'

The office was only a short distance and the men had Walt there in a flash. They hauled him in and laid him on the table. Ben began to give orders as he worked to familiarize himself with the layout of the room. 'Zane, get some water boiling on the stove.' He began to frantically pull open cabinets and drawers trying to locate what he needed.

'Water's already hot,' yelled Zane. 'I guess the doc keeps himself prepared.'

Ben poured some of the hot water into a basin to wash his hands.

'Zane, wash your hands. The rest of you leave the room.'

'We want to help too,' objected Smiley.

'I know you do, Smiley. I'll tell you what. The best thing you can do for Little Walt right now is ride out to the Dunkin place and see if you can hurry up the doc and explain the situation to him on the way back.

'You got it, Ben . . . I mean, Doc, but I ain't got a horse no more. I guess I'll have to take Walt's.'

Ben looked up as Smiley disappeared out the door. As he did, he noticed blood on Wes's shirt. 'You've been shot.'

'It's only a scratch. It can wait. You take care of Little Walt.'

Wes left the room and Zane closed the door.

★   ★   ★

A long hour had passed before Smiley got back with Doc Evans, who wasn't looking very happy. He went straight into the operating room and shut the door behind him. Ben was finishing up with Little Walt, who was still alive, but barely.

'Just who the hell are you, mister, and who in tarnation gave you the authority to operate on *my* table?'

Being a doctor himself, Ben wasn't a bit surprised at the reception, but he knew Doc Evans would understand once he explained himself. 'My name is Ben Dunn. I'm a doctor of surgery in Richmond, Virginia. I'm here visiting my uncle, Miles Hanley of the XO. I'm afraid I didn't get permission to use your table and I apologize for that, but it was an emergency; a matter of life and death . . .'

Zane broke into the conversation. 'Doc, you know me, and you know the rest of the men from the XO and that includes Little Walt here. Ben saved his life and this is the thanks he gets?'

Ben smiled across at his companion, grateful for the compliment. 'It's OK, Zane. Doc Evans has every right to be upset. I made a mess of his operating room and I used it without his permission. I've apologized for that.'

'Well,' replied Doc Evans. 'No harm done. I appreciate the professional courtesy and the apology. How's your man doing?' The doc leaned over the table to get a closer look. 'That's some mighty fine looking stitch work there, if I do say so myself.' Turning his attention back to Zane, he continued. 'You may leave the room now, Zane. I'll take over from here.'

'Thank you, doctor,' replied Ben. 'He seems to be stable at the moment. His left lung is partially collapsed. It was punctured by a piece of rib that was chipped off when the bullet hit it. I opened him up a bit and removed the slug and the piece of rib. I did what I could to repair the damage before I closed the incision. It's not a pretty sight. He's holding his own right now, but only time will tell. At least his breathing isn't so labored. Again, I do apologize for taking over your office like this. I never would have done it if I thought it could have waited. This is quite a setup you have here for such a small town.'

'Fort Scott ain't so small, and I do keep up on the latest medical advancements. I noticed when I came in that there's a man in the outer room with blood on his shirt. You might as well tend to him also.'

Ben and Doc Evans moved Little Walt to a bed where he could be tended to during his recovery, then Ben stepped out to get Wes.

'Come on in here Wes, you're next.'

Zane, Wes and Smiley all stood up. 'Not so fast, Ben. You owe us an explanation,' answered Wes.

Ben was on the spot, so he decided to come clean right then. 'I think you're right, boys. I do at that.'

The boys sat back down as Ben did his best to explain. 'My name is Ben Dunn and Miles Hanley, he's my uncle. I'm here because I'm a wanted man back in Virginia. Not wanted by the law, but wanted by a group of men, vigilantes, who are out to kill me.'

'Kill you? What on earth for?' asked Smiley.

'They want to kill me because of what I believe in, and because I operated on a Negro. He was beaten near to death for no other reason but that he walked across the path of a white woman. I saved his life, I took him into my home and nursed him back to health, but there were some men in town that didn't like what I did for the man. My home was burned to the ground and my patient and I escaped by the thinnest of margins. They came after me, but I escaped and came here until things calmed down enough for me to return home. I'm sorry I pretended to be a ranch hand, but I wanted to earn my keep.'

'We knew you weren't a ranch hand. You're too damn lousy at it. You must have figured we were on to you?' added Zane, with a smile.

'I figured so, but I do appreciate your

putting up with me. Well, anyhow, that's my story, now let me take a look at that shoulder, Wes.'

Ben cleaned up the wound and put a bandage over it. The bullet had just creased Wes's arm drawing a fair amount of blood, but not causing any real damage. A few stitches and he was as good as new.

'So, what's your plan now, Ben? Hopefully you're not coming back to work at the XO,' Smiley said with a laugh.

'No, I'm afraid my ranching days are over. I'm not cut out to be a ranch hand. I'm not really sure what I'm going to do now.'

Doc Evans interrupted. 'Well, I have an idea. This town is getting awful big for only one doctor and I'd love to be able to cut back on the amount of hours I'm putting in. I might be willing to share my office with you for a time. Evans and Dunn. Has a ring to it, don't you think?'

'Well, you know Doc, that sounds

like a good idea, at least for the time being. I don't have to think twice about it. I'll take you up on that offer. I'll need a day or two to collect my belongings from the XO and get settled here in town.'

'No problem, but you're not leaving this office until after you help me clean up this mess.'

'I wouldn't have it any other way, Doctor Evans.' replied Ben, with a smile.

'Oh please, let's get ourselves onto a first name basis here. My name's Marcus. Once we get this mess cleaned up we can work out the details over supper.'

Ben turned his attention back to the boys. 'I'll tell you what. If you boys want to stay the night in town, I'll pick up the tab for the horses and for a night at the boarding house. Then we'll all head back out to the XO in the morning.'

'Smiley never was one to pass up an opportunity when he saw one,' Wes piped up. 'Does that include drinks at the Hoof and Horn?' he asked.

'Why not, I'll pay for your drinks, but that's all. No extracurricular activities, if you know what I mean.'

'Extracurricular activities, no. What do you mean by that?' questioned Smiley.

Zane chuckled. 'He means he isn't going to pay for a woman or your gambling losses.'

'Oh, that. You got a deal, Ben.'

The boys took turns shaking Ben's hand and thanking him for what he had done for Little Walt, and for Wes too. As they headed out the door, Smiley exclaimed. 'Somehow, I gotta git me another horse.'

'A good horse will cost you near two hundred dollars, where do you think you're going to come up with that kind of money?' questioned Zane.

Smiley thought for a minute. 'Maybe I can get Ben to pay for it?'

They all had a good laugh at Smiley's joke, but what they didn't realize, was that he was serious.

3

On the Trail to Fort Scott

Sarah, Mac and Jason were making good time. The day had passed without incident and as night approached the three decided to make camp for the night. Sarah cooked up a meal of biscuits and beans with a generous helping of pork that Ellie had slipped into her bag before they left Fall River, and a pot of hot coffee was a good finishing touch. Few words were shared between Mac and Jason as they rode, but now by the fire they had a chance to talk a bit more.

'Mom says you own a big ranch outside of Fort Scott?'

Mac gave a chuckle as he gave a sideways glance over toward Sarah. 'My baby sister always did like to brag me up. I do live outside of town on a few

93

acres, but my business isn't ranching. Well, I take that back. It used to be ranching up until about a year ago, when I sold off my herd and started brokering cattle as they came up the Shawnee. Unfortunately for me, most of the older ranchers and farmers around here remember all too well the trouble Texas cattle coming up the Shawnee caused about twenty-odd years back, and the younger ones, they've at least heard about it from their parents. Seems opening it back up also opened up a lot of old memories along with it. Not long after the Shawnee went back into use, talk of a blockade started up. I ignored it, thinking it would blow over, but I'm afraid I was mistaken, and now the trail's been closed off once again. So, for now, I'm pretty much out of business. Seems all the cattle from Texas are coming up west of here now, over around Dodge City. So I've been forced to start raising my own herd again just to make ends meet.'

'There seems to be a lot more cows coming into the territory,' Jason ventured. 'We're seeing quite a few this year around my place, well, my old place I guess. But you're right, most are coming up into Dodge City. The railyards are busier than ever. I was going to see about finding some work there since I'm no longer in school, but Ma says I'm too young and Jim wouldn't have any part of it either. He said I was needed at home, but that was just an excuse so he wouldn't have to do any work. That man's worthless.' The belligerence returned and was obvious in his countenance when he looked across at his father; the challenge clear. 'Since you didn't go back and kill him, someday I just might.'

'Now, Jason,' scolded Sarah. 'What kind of talk is that? Jim may be a lot of things, and I agree worthless may be among them, but he's not worth risking a rope around your neck.'

'No one would hang me for putting a bullet in him. They'd probably pin a medal on my chest.'

The mother mode kicked in, and Sarah was determined to end the nonsense. 'That's enough, Jason, I'll hear no more of it. I think it's time we get some sleep.'

Mac was watching his son's face; could see the boy was on the prod. He decided not to make an issue of it; not now. 'Sarah's right,' he said, throwing the dregs of his coffee into the fire. He kept his tone neutral. 'We have a long ride ahead of us tomorrow if we expect to make it to Fort Scott before sundown.'

Sarah and Mac moved away from the fire to get some shuteye. Jason stayed up, poking at the hot embers with a stick, thinking back on all that had transpired over the past week, and at what might lay ahead.

The following morning after a hearty breakfast of flapjacks, eggs and hot coffee, Mac and Jason saddled up the horses. As Jason threw his saddle over his horse, the axe handle slipped out of the scabbard he carried it in. Mac picked it up. 'Why do you carry an axe handle?' He asked.

'Because I don't own a gun.'

'I don't think you can do much damage with this ol' thing.'

'Well, I'm afraid it's all I've got for now, so it'll have to do,' snapped Jason as he grabbed the handle from Mac and slipped it back into the scabbard.

'Why are you such an angry young man, Jason?'

Jason turned and faced Mac. 'Angry, I'll tell you why I'm angry. I never knew my real mother, I was abandoned at birth by my real father, and up until last week I was beat almost daily by the man I was left with and Sarah let it happen. I'm truly grateful that she finally did what she did to get us out of that situation, but I'm a bit lost and confused right now. I don't know you. I don't know where I'm going, and I don't know if I even went to stick around once I get there. Does that answer your question?' he ground out.

Mac was almost tempted to take a step back, but changed his mind and stood his ground. 'I guess it does. I only hope you give me the opportunity to make it up to you, and maybe help you try and figure things out.'

'We'll see how it goes.' Jason finished cinching his saddle and mounted up.

It was late in the afternoon, about an hour's ride from Fort Scott when they approached four riders coming in the opposite direction. As they closed in on them, Mac recognized who they were.

'Howdy boys, how are things at the XO?'

Zane spoke up, 'Why, if it isn't Mac Shepard. Haven't seen much of you lately. How the heck are you?

Mac nodded in greeting and pulled up. He took off his stetson, using his elbow to swipe of the leather-banded interior. 'I'm holding my own. I managed to pick up a few hundred head last week, but I'm afraid I'm done for as a broker, so right now I'm looking to get my own herd built up.'

He smoothed he hair and settled the hat back on his head.

'A few hundred head, you say? I know they didn't come up the Shawnee; it's blocked off. How'd they get here?'

Mac grinned. 'I reckon they got off the trail somewhere and I was lucky enough to be in their path.'

'Lucky, I guess! The only Texas cattle I've seen in these parts lately have a stink to them. Brokerin' rustled cattle is a bit risky. I'd be careful if I were you,' the man warned.

'The brands were good,' Mac responded, 'I made sure of that. Hey, I'm sorry for being so rude. Let me introduce you to my sister, Sarah and her son . . . no, my son, Jason.

'Didn't know you had a son?' replied Smiley.

'It's a long story. I'll tell it to you some time.'

'I can't wait to hear it.'

'Sarah, Jason these here boys work for the XO. This here is Wes, Smiley,

Zane and their newest man, Ben. Where's Little Walt today'?

'Man, you talk about having a story to tell,' replied Zane. 'We've got you beat, hands down. Little Walt was shot yesterday, and Doc Evans was out of town, but as luck would have it, Ben here turns out to be a doctor. He saved Walt's life.'

'Your new man's a doctor?'

'You better believe it, and a damn good one at that. Doc Evans and him cut a deal. They're going to share an office in town.'

'Well, sounds like you're going to be down a man or two for awhile. I happen to know someone who might be looking for a job if you're interested. He's green, but a hard worker.'

'He don't wear no ten-gallon hat, does he?' asked Wes.

That got the rest of the boys to laughing and even Ben had to chuckle some.

'No, but if you're hiring, Jason here might be interested.' He waved in the general direction of is boy.

'I'm sure we'll be needing to replace Little Walt for a spell,' replied Zane. 'Why don't you and Jason come on out to the house tomorrow and we'll talk, if that's OK with Jason here, of course.'

Jason stepped his horse forward toward the men. 'Why wait until tomorrow? I can head back with you now.'

'Well now, there's a man who knows what he wants. I like that quality. I guess we could do that, if it's OK with the two of you?'

Before Mac or Sarah had a chance to speak up, Jason broke in. 'Look Mac, your business is down and I don't think you can afford two more mouths to feed. Ma, Mac obviously doesn't have work for me or he wouldn't have asked these men about putting me to work, and they're willing to give me a chance. It makes no sense to ride all the way into town just to turn around again in the morning and ride back out. Mac has already been away for four days,

I'm sure he'd rather not take another day to take me out to the XO.'

'The kid puts up a good argument, Mac,' stated Zane.'

'What do you think, Sarah,' asked Mac.

'Why, I don't know. This is all so sudden . . . ' The words drifted off into nothingness.

Jason sensed his mother's hesitancy, and it somehow made him feel guilty; as if he were deserting her, when, in consideration of the circumstances, it was actually the sensible thing to do. *For all of them.* 'Ma, I'm goin'. Just make it easier and say yes.'

Sarah began to cry. She knew she would lose her son some day, but she just didn't expect it to be like this, on the trail and so sudden like. She had wanted time for him to heal; time to get to know his father; and it was all being taken away.

'I'll come see you on weekends, I promise,' Jason said, attempting to sweeten the pot.

'You better,' she replied.

Composed, Sarah wiped her nose and stepped down from her horse. 'Come down here, young man.'

Jason stepped down off his horse and Sarah grabbed him up in her arms and hugged him hard as she continued to cry anew.

'Now that's touching,' commented Smiley, as he wiped the tears from his eyes.

'I didn't know you were so sentimental,' replied Wes.

'Damn right I am. And you better not ever hold it against me.'

Sarah took a step back as she kept her hands firmly on Jason's shoulders. She took a deep breath and lifted off his hat. She brushed his hair back with her hand and set his hat on nice and straight. She kissed him softly on the cheek. The lump in her throat made it difficult to speak, but she was determined to do this right, so through her tears and a trembling heart, she gave Jason her blessing. 'You're no longer a boy, Jason. You're a young man, and I know your life hasn't been easy up to this point. I hope your trail forward will be smooth and life will be kind. You certainly deserve it. Now go, I'll see you on the weekend.'

She climbed back on her horse and rode down the trail alone.

Mac quickly finished up with the men and said his good-bys to Jason, then left to catch up with Sarah, who was sobbing as she rode.

★   ★   ★

As the XO boys rode up to the main house they could see Miles sitting in his favorite rocker smoking his pipe and enjoying a quiet Sunday afternoon. Smiley yelled out. 'Boss, you won't believe it. Wes brought home another stray.'

Miles got up and walked to the steps where the men had pulled up. 'And what have we got here. Where's Little Walt?'

All the men started talking at one time and Miles wasn't understanding a word of what was being said. 'Whoa, now, hold on. You sound like a bunch of old ladies at a sewing bee. Zane, what's going on? Who's this young man and where's Little Walt.'

'It's been a wild weekend, Miles. Little Walt is still in town at Doc Evans's place. He got shot real bad. We didn't think he was going to make it, but it turns out, this here greenhorn of a ranch hand you hired is a mighty damn fine doctor. Doc Evans was out of town delivering a baby, so we just took over his office, and Ben here surprised the hell out of all of us and patched up Little Walt as good as new, and sewed up a hole in Wes's arm too.'

Miles took a puff off his pipe as he took in what Zane had just told him. 'Is that the way it was, Ben?'

'Well basically, except for the part about Little Walt being as good as new. He's still alive, but it's touch and go right now. The bullet hit one of his ribs and a splinter punctured one of his lungs. I got the bullet and the splinter out and did my best to repair the lung. Now it's up to him. He'll be under my care for a few weeks, at least. And that's the other part that Zane left off. I'm turning in my slip. I'll be assisting Doc Evans in town now. I came clean with the boys here. They know my whole story. I just came back to pick up my belongings and I'll be heading out in the morning.'

'Well let's hope Little Walt pulls through. I'm sure he'll have a much better chance with both you *and* Doc Evans at his side. Now tell me about this here stray you boys brought home, Wes. I see this one ain't wearing a ten-gallon hat.'

'No sir, he ain't wearin' no ten-gallon hat, but he is green. Seems to be a good enough kid though. I think he'll do just fine. We ran into Mac Shepard on our way home. He was on his way back from Fall River with his sister and his son.'

'So Mac has a son? I never knew that.'

'He's Mac's son all right, but his sister raised him from an infant.'

Now that Miles had a better understanding, he turned his attention to the kid.

'So, what's your name son?'

'Jason, sir.'

'No now, don't be sir'n me. If you're going to work here at the XO, you best get used to calling me Miles. So, you're from Fall River are you?'

'No sir . . . I mean, Miles. I'm from Wichita. My ma and I made it to Fall River where Mac met up with us. We were heading out to his place, but he doesn't seem to have much work right now on account of the Shawnee trail being blockaded. So when I heard you were going to be short handed, I took the opportunity to ask for a job, and Zane here seems to think I'll do just fine.'

Miles walked down the steps and over to Jason. Reaching up, he shook his hand. 'If Zane thinks you'll work out, then I think you'll work out. Welcome to the XO, son. Why don't you boys get these horses taken care of and then clean yourselves up for supper, and show Jason his bunk while you're at it. Ben, before you call it a night, come see me.'

Zane lingered back while the men headed for the barn so he could talk to Miles alone.

'Mac let it slip that he picked up several hundred head of Texas longhorns the other day.'

'What, how the hell did he do that? Does he still have 'em?'

'No, he said he brokered them off.'

'How did he get them?'

'He said they wandered off the Chisholm and as luck would have it, landed right in his lap.'

'There was no luck to it. There's no legitimate cattle coming this direction. We all know that.'

'I warned him, but he assured me the brands were good. I know he's hurting right now, afraid he might lose his place.'

'I feel for him, Zane, but we've all worked too hard to let Texas fever get another foothold around these parts. I'm not going to let him endanger our livelihood just because he's about to go under.'

'So, what do you think?'

'I think we need to keep an eye on him, maybe I'll head out to his place one of these days and we'll have ourselves a talk. Until then I think I'll at least make the sheriff aware of the situation. Thanks for filling me in, Zane. Now go get yourself cleaned up for supper.'

★   ★   ★

After the men had eaten their supper and pestered Jason with a million questions about himself, Wichita, the Chisholm trail and the railyards, they decided to teach Jason how to play poker. Ben took the opportunity to head up to the house and have a talk with Miles, who was sitting in his customary spot on the front porch enjoying the cool summer evening.

'Ben, have a seat. Care for a smoke?'

'No thanks, Miles. I don't smoke.'

'Don't smoke? Why that's mighty unusual for a man not to smoke. I myself enjoy the pleasure of a good bowl of tobacco on an evening such as this. So tell me, how in the hell did Little Walt manage to get himself shot?'

'It wasn't anything he did. We were just leaving the livery when we were approached by two men wanting to know if we were blue or gray. Little Walt spouted off that he was a yank and proud of it. It must have riled them, 'cuz that's when they pulled their guns and started shooting. Wes caught a round in the shoulder. Just a flesh wound really. It only took a few stitches, but Little Walt caught one square in the chest. I did what I could for him, but he's in a bad way right now. It could go either way for him.'

'So, you're a good doctor, are you?'

'I had a good practice in Richmond, but I made the mistake of letting my political views be known by giving a helping hand to a Negro, and I paid the price for it.'

'You know, Ben. Sometimes there's a high price to pay for doing the right thing. It's never a mistake to help a man in need, no matter what the color of his skin. You've chosen a noble profession and you can always be proud of that.'

'That may be true, Miles, but look at what it got me.'

'You're looking at it all wrong, Ben. It got you out of that big city back east and out here into the wide open where a man can ride for miles and see nothing but tall grass and cattle . . . and maybe a buffalo or two.'

'I'm afraid I haven't seen any buffalo.'

'You will, that is if that man Cody doesn't shoot them all first.'

'Cody? I don't think I know him.'

'Stick around here long enough and you will. So what do you think of this

111

new kid, Jason. He looks like he might be a handful with that red hair and all.'

'Now that sounds a bit like judging a man by the color of his skin, doesn't it?'

'We're talking hair here, not skin.'

'Oh, I see. Well, I think he'll do just fine in spite of his red hair. He has to be better than me.'

'Well, that ain't sayin' much, Ben . . . no offense.'

'None taken,' replied Ben with a chuckle. 'I know I'm not cut out for ranch work.'

'So how long do you plan on stayin' around these parts?'

'I'm waiting to hear from my parents, they're suppose to let me know when it's safe to return.'

'As far as I'm concerned, I hope they take their time. You're already makin' friends here. Maybe you'll decide to stay when that time comes. It's gettin' late. I think I'm goin' to call it a night. I'll see you in the mornin'. Don't let me forget I'm holdin' some money for you.'

'Oh you don't have to worry about

that. I'll get it from you when I say my good-bys in the morning.'

'I figured so. Goodnight, Ben.'

Miles wandered back into the house, but Ben sat on the porch a while longer, soaking in the splendor of a million stars on a clear summer night.

★ ★ ★

It was early the following morning, Ben was up for breakfast with the rest of the hands. He lingered in the yard and said his good-bys as the men went off to do their chores. Once his bags were packed he had a few final words with Miles before heading into town to meet up with Doc Evans. As he rode out of the yard, Miles called out a final word.

'Just remember, Ben. You're welcome back here any time . . . to visit, not to work.'

They both cracked a smile. One final wave from Ben and they both turned to go about their business.

Zane had Jason work around the

barn for the day, forking out the stalls among other general cleaning chores. He wanted to see if the boy could be trusted to work on his own. He didn't want his men playing nursemaid to the boy, not that they would.

Jason wanted to prove his worth, so he kept his mouth shut and did as he was told. It's not like he had never cleaned out a stall before. He'd been doing it ever since he could handle a fork. The good thing is that he didn't have to worry about getting beat if something wasn't quite right, and to top it off, he was getting paid to do it.

The following day Zane put him with the rest of the hands as they worked the cattle. By the end of the week he had blended in. The men took a liking to him and quickly considered him one of the boys.

Each Friday was payday at the XO, and the boys usually made their way into town the following morning to relax and enjoy themselves at the Hoof and Horn, which they planned to do this week as well, but first they wanted to check in on Little Walt to see how he was holding up.

As they all rode into town the following morning a couple of the boys decided to have a little fun with Jason.

'So tell me Jason,' asked Zane. 'Have you ever had a drink of really good whiskey?'

'No, I've never had a whiskey of any kind,' he replied.

'Oh come on now. You mean to tell me you never took a snort from your daddy's bottle when he wasn't lookin'?' teased Smiley. 'How about a woman? Have you ever had yourself a woman? I'll bet not. I'll bet you ain't never had a whiskey or a woman, have ya?'

Jason didn't like the teasing. He closed up on Smiley and shoved him so hard he almost fell off his horse. Wes thought that was pretty funny until Smiley came back at Jason in a huff and Jason pulled the axe handle he carried out of his rifle scabbard. Smiley, not to be outdone, reached for his gun. Just

115

then Zane squeezed in between the two of them.

'OK, that'll be enough you two. Jason, put that damn stick away. You need to learn how to take a joke. We were only funnin' ya'.'

'I don't take to being made fun of!' snapped Jason.

'Well you got a mighty short fuse there, boy. It'll get you into trouble some day if you're not careful, especially in the Hoof and Horn. I won't fun ya' anymore,' replied Smiley. 'But if you ever pull that stick on me again, you can expect to be gaggin' on it.' He rode on up ahead, alongside Wes.

Later that afternoon as the men rode in to the livery, Jason decided he would continue out to Mac's place to see his ma. 'I don't think I'm going to head in with you all right now, I need to see my ma first.'

'Oh, come on Jason, why don't you hang around with us for awhile. We wanted to buy you your first drink.'

'And maybe even a woman,' laughed

Smiley, obviously forgetting the promise he had made earlier.

After much coercion, Jason finally relented. 'OK, one whiskey.'

'And maybe a couple hands of poker,' added Wes. 'Besides, you gotta go with us to see Little Walt, so I can tease him about how you have his job . . . if that's OK with you?'

'And let's not forget about Ben. We need to see how he's holding up too,' added Zane.

So the boys unsaddled their horses and made sure they had feed and water. After making arrangements with the stableman to stay the night in the loft, they headed over to the new 'Evans and Dunn' office to say hi to Ben and see how Little Walt was doing.

Little Walt was making good progress. Ben had done a top rate job at patching him up. He was sitting up and his breathing was much better, but he was still mighty sore from the whole ordeal.

'Another week and I'll be as good as new,' he teased.

'More like a month,' replied Ben.

'Don't you worry none, Walt. We got ourselves a real good replacement,' teased Wes as he slapped Jason on the back. 'This kid can work circles around you. Why, we don't care if you never come back.'

'Gee, thanks for the vote of confidence,' replied Walt.

'Oh, don't look so rejected, Walt. You know I'm just teasing you . . . don't you?'

'I figured so, but I ain't got a wife, so I got to get some sympathy wherever I can find it.'

'Well how about if we send one of the girls from the Hoof and Horn over. We'll make sure she gives you all the sympathy you want.'

'OK, that'll be enough, boys. What Walt needs most of all right now is rest, not sympathy', interjected Ben.

'You're quite the spoiler, you know that, Ben.'

'Sorry, Wes. That's my job.'

After the boys had a chance to talk

118

with Ben for a spell, and see for themselves that Little Walt was on the mend, they headed over to the Hoof and Horn.

'You boys be careful,' cautioned Ben. 'I don't want to be pulling lead out of any more XO boys tonight, or any night for that matter.'

'Don't you worry about us, Ben. But then that don't mean we won't be sending any business your way,' replied Wes, with a laugh as he walked out the door.

As the men pushed their way through the bat wings of the Hoof and Horn, they were immediately hailed up to the bar by Ira, the bartender. 'Well, it's about time you XO boys showed up. Have you been over to see Little Walt yet? I've been stoppin' in every morning on my way here. He seems to be a little better every day. And who would have thought that that dandy who walked in here with the ten-gallon hat would turn out to be the doc who saved his life. You just never know about people now, do ya?'

'Boy, you got that right, Ira,' replied Zane. 'You just never know how someone might turn out.'

'Who's the young feller hiding back behind you there? Step on out from behind this big lug and show yourself. That's better. How do you do there, young man? My name's Charles, Charles O'Donnell, but my friends call me Ira, and any friend of these boys, is a friend of mine.'

Jason reached forward to shake Ira's hand. 'How do you do Ira, I'm Jason.'

'Jason here's from Wichita,' added Zane. 'He's working for the XO now. In fact, we're breaking him in tonight. We're buying him his very first drink, so why don't you set a bottle of your best whiskey up here.'

'I only have one kind of whiskey, and since this here is my establishment, I'll be the one to buy the kid his first drink.'

Ira set a shot glass up on the bar in front of Jason and filled it to the top. He set the bottle down and looked up at Jason.

'Well, there you go, boy. What are ya' waitin' for?'

The XO boys all stood in close to Jason, anticipating a good laugh.

Jason picked up the glass and put it to his lips.

'Whoa, hold on there, boy. That ain't milk, and that ain't how you drink whiskey. You pick it up and throw it back all at once, so it slides on down yer throat as smooth as silk.'

'More like burlap,' joked Smiley.

Jason picked up the shot glass and gulped the whiskey down in one quick swallow, and as expected, Ira and all the XO boy had a good laugh as Jason's reaction to the drink was just as expected, a loss of breath as it burned its way down to his stomach.

Ira handed Zane a new bottle and the boys found themselves a table where they started up a friendly game of poker.

The boys played a few hands and had a few drinks. It was late in the afternoon when Jason decided he had better make his way to Mac's place to see his ma.

'Well, I want to thank you all for introducing me to the Hoof and Horn and Ira's whiskey. I'm afraid I need to find my way out to Mac's place before my ma begins to worry about me. How do I get there?'

'Well that's as easy as can be,' answered Zane. 'Head north out of town. You'll run into his place in about thirty minutes. Come back into town tomorrow before two and we'll ride back to the XO together.'

As Jason got up to leave, he looked over at Smiley. 'Hey, Smiley. I'd like to apologize for pulling my redeemer out on you this morning. I've been teased and tormented most of my life over one thing or another and I'm afraid I haven't been in the mood to take any more of it for quite some time now. You're my friend and I should have known you were only funnin' me.'

'I'm still your friend,' replied Smiley. 'I appreciate the kind words, but I still mean what I said to you, about that stick.

'Why do you carry that thing anyways, and why do you call it your 'Redeemer'?'

'It's a long story. I'll tell it to you some time, but right now I need to be going.'

'Well I like stories and I'll be expecting to hear it some day.'

'It's a deal,' replied Jason as he headed for the door.

Just as he was about to leave the saloon, the bat wings flew open and in walked Wiley Strome. He stood in front of the doorway blocking him from leaving. Wiley was a young kid, not more than twenty. He was a big talker who liked to bring attention to himself. The gun he carried was more for show and threatening people, than for real use. Wes had accused him on more than one occasion of not being able to hit the broad side of a barn, and had even challenged him to a shooting contest to prove his point, but Wiley kept brushing him off. The XO boys knew he could be trouble and expected something might happen when he blocked Jason's way out.

'Well, well, who let the kid in here. Are you lost son?' Wiley spied the red hair sticking out from under Jason's hat and continued with his badgering. 'And what have we here?' Wiley reached over and grabbed Jason's hat off his head. 'Would you look at that! Somebody get me a bucket of water. I think this boy's head is on fire.' Before Wiley had time to laugh at his own joke, Jason caught him with a mean right hook to the side of the head. It stunned him, but didn't put him down. Wiley grabbed Jason by the throat and shoved him up against the wall. He pulled his gun and held it up to Jason's head. 'You're going to wish you had never done that, boy.'

Suddenly Wiley felt the cold steel of a gun barrel pressing against the back of his own head.

'I don't think you want to do that, Wiley,' cautioned Zane. 'You so much as breathe hard on that boy, I'll blow your brains to kingdom come. Now put that gun back where it belongs and be quick about it.'

Wiley holstered his gun and let go of Jason. Zane removed his gun from the back of Wiley's head. As he did, Jason reached over and grabbed Wiley's gun and held the barrel against his chin. Wiley stood frozen.

'What the hell are you doing, boy!' yelled Zane.

Slowly, Jason pressed the gun a little tighter against Wiley's chin. 'Don't ever tease me, and don't *ever* threaten me again, or I swear by everything that's good and holy, I'll kill you.' Jason shoved the gun back into Wiley's holster and stormed out through the bat wings leaving them flapping in his wake.

'What the hell was that all about?' questioned Wiley. 'I was just funnin' the kid.'

'Don't mess with him, Wiley. He's a good kid, but he has a few issues. Don't know what they are, yet, but I know he doesn't like being teased, so go easy on him.'

'That kid's a hothead all right. Red hair, hothead, get it?' Wiley couldn't help but laugh at his own cleverness, but then abruptly stopped and rubbed his jaw where Jason had punched him.

'That kid packs quite a punch, I know that much.' Turning to Ira he placed his order. 'Ira, draw me a beer, will you.' Turning back to Zane, he looked him in the eye and with a hint of seriousness in his voice, he commented. 'Don't ever let that kid get his own gun, I'm afraid he might use it on someone some day, and I don't believe it'll be in self defense.'

'You may be right, Wiley, you may be right.'

Zane went back to the table with the boys. 'I don't know about that boy. If he keeps this up, he may be more than I want to handle.'

'Oh come on Zane. It was the whiskey talkin',' answered Wes. 'Some people get mean when they drink, and he has had a few, and we all know he doesn't like being messed with, so give the kid a break.'

After leaving the saloon, Jason headed straight for the livery and retrieved his horse. Finding the road north, he headed toward Mac's place. It was a pleasant afternoon and Jason rode slow as the alcohol had had some effect on him. He soon came to what he assumed was Mac's ranch. He passed several large, empty corrals before seeing the house in the distance. As he rode up to the gate, Sarah came bounding off the porch to meet him. 'Jason, I thought maybe you weren't coming?'

'I told you I'd see you on the weekends. The boys wanted to buy me a drink before I came out.'

'Buy you a drink? They better not have! You're too young for that. What kind of men are these, giving alcohol to a young boy!'

'Ma, they're my friends and I'm not a young boy, I'm almost fifteen, so let's drop it. How've you been? Looks like Mac has a nice place here. Not many cows though.'

'He's having a tough time of it right now with all the Texas cattle coming up the Chisholm these days. Seems like the man you work for had a big hand in shutting down the Shawnee. I'm surprised Mac is still friends with him.'

Jason had dismounted and was leading his horse toward the hitching rail. 'You know the Texas cattle were spreading a deadly disease to the cattle around here. We heard about that back in Wichita. The ranchers around here did what they had to do to protect their herds.'

Sarah suppressed a small frown. 'That doesn't make it any easier on Mac. With no cattle to buy he has no income other than what he makes off his own cows, and what few cattle manage to make it around the blockade. He's thinking about going back to Wichita or maybe Abilene and getting a job with one of the brokers back there. I'm worried if he does go back to Wichita, he might have a run in with Jim.'

Jason's eyes narrowed, a slow smile coming at his mother's words. 'You're right, maybe he'll kill him.' He chuckled aloud. 'I think you should encourage him to go,' he said mischievously.'

'Jason, don't talk like that.' Sarah chided.

Jason shrugged, the whiskey he had consumed making him not give a damn about what he was thinking. 'Why not? I hate that man.'

As the two stood talking, a buggy came up the road and stopped in front of the house. It was Doctor Dunn.

'Good afternoon, Sarah, Jason, It's a beautiful day today, don't you agree?'

'Yes, it's a fine day, Doctor Dunn,' replied Sarah.

'Oh please, I think we can dispense with the formalities out here, please call me Ben. Can you tell me if Mac is about?'

'Yes, as a matter of fact he is. Jason, Mac is out in the barn, would you be so kind as to go fetch him for Doctor . . . I mean Ben.'

Jason headed for the barn, giving Ben and Sarah a chance to get better acquainted.

'Last I seen you, you were bawling your eyes out. Have you recovered?'

'I'm getting used to it. I never thought I'd be alone at this point in my life.'

'I completely understand. I left everything I owned and everyone I knew back in Richmond. I'm hoping I'll be able to return before too long.'

'I'm afraid I don't know what I'm hoping for. A fresh start, I guess.'

'Well, if you plan on being in town much, maybe we'll be seeing more of each other before I head back to Richmond.'

'I think I'd like that, Ben.'

The two continued with their small talk until Mac and Jason met back up with them.

'Well hello there, Ben. What brings you out this way today?' inquired Mac.

'Oh, nothing special. I just thought I'd take some time to get to know my

130

neighbors, and to check up on Sarah. She was mighty down the last time I seen her, but I see the color is back in her cheeks. That's always a good sign. How's the cattle business going for you?'

'I'm afraid it's not going too well. I'm not getting a lick of business. It's all heading into the stock yards in Abilene.'

'That's what I hear. I know when I was out at the XO, they were pretty happy that the Texas cattle were using the Chisholm and that the Shawnee had pretty much dried up. I'm surprised you're still on speaking terms with them, considering they played a large part in this whole affair, and it seems to have put you out of business.'

'I happen to like Miles and the men who ride for the XO, and that includes Jason here, now. It's not their fault those longhorns are carrying a disease that's killing off the cattle up here. They're just trying to protect their interests. You know, that trail was blocked off twenty some years ago for the very same reason. When it opened up again last year, I thought I'd try and make a go of it as a broker. Unfortunately, the blockade was put back in place, If that hadn't happened, they'd be the ones suffering, not me. It's just the luck of the draw.'

'It's nice to see you take it so well. I hope things work out for you. I'd hate to see you and Sarah have to leave Fort Scott.'

'Hopefully it won't come to that, but I'll do what I have to do.'

'I understand that all too well.'

Sarah interrupted the conversation. 'Enough talk about leaving Fort Scott. I just got here and if I have to take a job in town to help my brother make ends meet, then that's exactly what I'll do. And speaking of working, I've been cooking most of the afternoon. Won't you please stay for supper with us. If I recall, the last we met, you were on your way to gather your things from the XO. You now have an office in town, is that right? I'd love to hear all about it.'

'Well, I'm actually sharing an office with Doc Evans for now. Like I said, I'm not expecting to stick around too long, and the situation is working out well. But I will stay long enough to have supper with you, that's for sure.'

'Then it's settled. You men can take care of the horse and wash up. I'll set an extra plate.'

* * *

For the next several weeks things were pretty quiet. Jason was working out well for the XO and Little Walt had recovered from his wound enough to where he left Ben's care and went to stay at the XO. Mac was still having a hard time of it and Sarah, true to her word, went into town to find work. She checked with the general store and two restaurants, but nobody was looking to hire.

She was about to give up for the day when she ran into Ben as he was coming out of the barbershop. He doffed his hat and made no move to step out of her way. There was a brief, awkward silent, and Ben was the first to speak.

'Why Sarah, how are you? I haven't seen you for a spell, although I do still think about that delicious peach pie you served up for desert when last we met. What brings you into town today?'

Sarah's cheeks colored. It had been a long time since a man so close to her own age had spoken to her so politely; and she felt like a schoolgirl. 'Well thank you, Ben. I enjoyed serving it to you. It was quite a pleasant evening. I've come to town in search of work, but I'm afraid I haven't had much luck.'

'I see, so Mac is still having a hard time of it, is he?'

Sarah frowned. 'Yes, I'm afraid so. I'm real concerned he may be serious about heading back to Wichita unless I find something to help him make ends meet. Right now, I'm just an extra burden to him, and it bothers me.'

Ben reached out to take Sarah's arm,

guiding her out of the sun and into the shadows beneath a porch roof. 'It's funny we should meet today. Doc Evans and I were just this morning discussing the need of finding someone to help around the office.' Smiling, he hesitated; mischief deep in his eyes. 'Do you know how to boil water?'

The question surprised Sarah, and it showed in her face. 'Boil water? Are you fooling with me? Of course I can boil water.' Then, realizing he was teasing, she swatted his arm.

Ben's grin widened, and he rubbed at his forearm as if it really hurt. 'OK, here's a harder question. Do you faint at the sight of blood?

Realizing he was serious, she gave him a straight answer. 'I've seen my share of blood and I have never fainted, nor have I been nauseated by the sight.'

Ben nodded. 'Well then, I think we may have a job for you. Of course, I'll need to discuss it with Doc Evans first. I'll let you know tomorrow, that is, if you're truly interested.'

Sarah didn't even have to think about it. 'Why yes, Ben, I'm very interested. Thank you.'

He was visibly relieved. 'Then I'll let you know tomorrow.'

A bit of small talk ensued and as Sarah finished up with a polite good-by, Ben asked if he might accompany her to her buggy.

'Why yes, Ben. I would very much like that,' she replied.

They continued their conversation until they reached Sarah's buggy. Ben helped her up and as Sarah was leaving, Ben called out. 'I'll let you know about the job, tomorrow.'

As he watched her ride away, Ben couldn't help but notice what a fine looking woman she was. Sarah turned her head for one final look as she continued down the street toward home. Ben couldn't help but smile as he slowly walked back to his office, suddenly realizing what a fine day it was.

4

Tobias Trouble

It was a Saturday night. Jason, Smiley, Wes and an older trail rider who went by the name of 'Tex' sat at the corner table in the Hoof and Horn. They had been playing poker for a couple of hours, and Jason, who had turned out to be quite adept at playing the game was ahead. The final hand of the night had seen the pot grow quite large. Wes and Smiley had folded, but Tex and Jason continued raising each other until Tex finally called and with a smile on his face and thoughts of sweet success, laid down three jacks with a flourish.

Jason looked at the hand and slowly laid down his own. 'I'm afraid I have you beat there, Tex. I have three tens . . . and two little ladies to boot.'

'Why that can't be,' cried Tex. 'You're

just a kid. I'll bet you don't even shave yet!'

'I may not shave, but I know how to play poker. The pot's mine! Do you have a problem with that?'

Tex was upset, but he was no fool. With Smiley and Wes sitting at the table, he grabbed up what little money he had left and called it a night. He would wait for another time and place to get his money back. 'We'll meet again,' he told Jason as he left the table.

'Bring more money,' Jason replied as he collected his winnings and bought a round of drinks for his friends.

Not anticipating his good fortune at the table, Jason had paid for a night in the livery loft with the rest of the XO boys. It wasn't uncommon for the stableman to rent out sleeping space in the loft to whoever wanted an inexpensive place to lay their head for the night. It just so happened that Tex was sleeping in the loft that night as well.

About an hour after the card game

had ended, the boys decided to call it a night and wandered down to the livery. Tex was already in the loft when the boys came in. They lit a lamp, but kept the flame low as not to disturb several others who were already asleep. Tex kept his head down so he wouldn't be noticed. He took note of where Jason hung his hat for the night before the light was put out. After what Tex figured was enough time for the men to be asleep, and hoping he had the added benefit of some heavy drinking on his side, he ever so slowly made his way over to where Jason was sleeping. Little did Tex know that over the years, Jason had developed a habit of being a light sleeper on account of he never knew when his 'father' was going to come home drunk and pull him out of bed to beat him. Old habits die hard, and tonight was no different. Jason had sensed someone moving in the loft and laid still. When he realized that someone was at his side, he figured they were after the money he had won earlier that evening. As soon as Jason felt a hand sliding into his pocket, he grabbed the stranger and began to tussle with him. The commotion woke up the rest of the men in the loft. Some began to yell for a light, not realizing what was going on. That didn't stop Jason and Tex from struggling with each other. Jason was quickly on his feet and just as a match was struck to light a lamp, Jason saw who it was and gave him a mighty shove that sent him backwards over the edge of the loft and to the floor below. All of the men scrambled to the edge and peered over just as the stableman stepped out from his quarters with a lighted lamp. There at his feet lay Tex, sprawled out on the floor. Blood was running from both his mouth and a deep gash on the back of his head. The stableman examined the body, then — looking up at the heads peering over the edge of the loft — he made the pronouncement, 'He's dead.'

'He was trying to steal my money,' shouted Jason as he looked around the room for the men to give some sign of agreement.

'I don't know what the scuffle was about, but I saw you push him over the edge,' answered one.

Even the boys from the XO had to agree they had only seen Jason push the man over the edge. The sheriff was summoned and an investigation was held. After hearing the story of Tex losing big to Jason at the poker table, it was determined that Tex was indeed after the money he had lost and Jason had acted in self defense. The following morning, after a sleepless night, Jason announced to the XO boys that he was planning to purchase a gun.

'It's about time,' replied Wes. 'Any self-respecting wrangler needs to have himself a gun, even if all he does with it was shoot an occasional jack rabbit. I think we should head over to the mercantile right now and take a look at what they have.'

Zane wasn't too keen on the idea of Jason owning a gun, but he kept his mouth shut and followed along as the boys made their way up the street to the Fort Scott Mercantile. If Jason was going to get himself a gun, he wanted to make sure he got a good one.

The boys entered the mercantile just as Andy Tobias — his friends called him Toby — had finished hanging a few new lanterns from hooks in the ceiling rafters. The men had congregated around the front counter where he normally had his guns on display.

'Well, well, if it isn't the whole danged XO outfit crowding around my display case. I guess you're not here for some fabric now, are you?'

'No sir, Toby, we're here to see what you've got for sale in the gun department,' replied Wes.

Toby perked right up. There was more profit to be made in selling firearms than dry goods. If a man bought a pistol, it only followed that he would buy a holster, belt and ammunition. 'Gun department, well, things are a bit scarce right now. I don't have any new guns, but I do have a real beauty in a used gun. That would be the .44 Colt you're looking at right now. Young Jason here has been drooling over that piece for the past two weeks now. Why every time he leaves, I have to clean the spittle off the glass. If you boys are all going to drool over this thing today, I'm going to hand you a rag and make you clean the glass yourselves,' he laughed good-naturedly.

'I'm not here to drool today, Toby. I got cash money,' cited Jason.

Toby's right eyebrow arched in surprise. 'Is that so? What did you do, rob a bank?'

'No sir, I won the money last night in a poker game.'

'That ain't quite the way I heard it,' Toby ventured. 'I heard talk around town this morning that you killed a man last night with your bare hands. What do you need a gun for?'

'Hey, that's unfair, Toby,' retorted Wes. 'Jason here was being robbed and he just shoved the man off of him. Tex hit his head in the fall. It was an accident.'

'I see,' replied Toby. 'Well, if you want that gun, it'll cost you twelve dollars.'

'Twelve dollars? You told me nine dollars last week. Now that's robbery,' cried Jason.

'That was last week, this is this week.' Afraid he might be missing out on the sale, he sweetened the deal. 'It comes with the holster and a box of cartridges.'

'I still think it's too much,' Jason complained.

'That's my price, take it or leave it,' Toby said. It was clear he was done dickering.

Jason inhaled, and nodded his head. 'I got the money and I'm tired of just looking at it, so I guess I'll take it.'

Toby reached into the case and brought out the gun. He handed it to Jason and Jason reluctantly gave him the twelve dollars.

He took the belt and strapped it on, sliding the pistol into the holster. He adjusted it so it hung low enough to be within easy reach with his elbow slightly cocked and fingers hovering comfortably above the walnut grip. Although this was the first time he had ever worn a pistol, he found something comforting in the weight against his thigh.

Satisfied, he removed the pistol from the holster and began feeding cartridges into the chamber. The gun belt was next; and Jason took his time placing the bullets into the twenty-five loops. The cartridges that remained, he put into his front pants pocket.

As the boys all stepped outside, Jason quickly stepped back in. He looked over at Toby, yelled out, 'You're a thief', and spit on the glass case before walking out the door.

Toby could be heard yelling something from inside the store as the boys headed down the street.

'What was that all about,' inquired Smiley.

'Oh, nothing, nothing at all,' Jason smirked.

By the time the boys made it back to the ranch, Zane was as jumpy as the horses, which was caused by Jason and Wes shooting off most of Jason's bullets as they took turns trying out the new gun.

Zane made a point of telling Miles all that had happened in town over the weekend. Miles called Jason up to the house after supper to have a talk with him.

'I hear you got into a tussle with someone over the weekend and he ended up dying at your hand,' Miles began, purposely trying hard to not sound judgmental.

'It was an accident, Miles,' Jason shrugged. 'I shoved him off the loft and he hit his head when he hit the ground. He was trying to rob me.'

'Accident or not, doesn't it bother you any that you killed a man?' Miles was watching Jason's face closely.

'He had it coming, as far as I'm concerned. No, it don't bother me.'

'I hear you did well at the poker table too.'

'Yes sir, good enough to buy me this here Colt.' Jason pulled the gun from its holster and handed it to Miles for a closer inspection.

'It's a nice piece; I owned one of these myself at one time.' He cleared his throat. 'I want to be certain that you understand there's to be no shooting around the house,' he finished as he handed the gun back to Jason. He felt a need to change the subject. 'How's your ma doing? I hear she took a job with Ben and Doc Evans.'

'Yes, but she's not there on the weekends.'

'So did you go out to see her?'

'No, I didn't have time this weekend. I'll try to make it out next time. Is that all?'

'I suppose it is.'

Jason headed back to the bunkhouse, drawing and reholstering his new pistol as he went. Miles watched him from the porch and wondered to himself how long it would be before Jason ended up behind bars, or worse.

The following morning, just after breakfast, Miles called Wes and Jason up to the house. 'You two hitch up the wagon. Toby should have some supplies in for us and I need the two of you to pick them up. I expect you back here by noon.'

The two boys hitched up the wagon and headed toward town. The ride was pretty boring until they came to a rocky spot. 'Hey, look there,' pointed Wes. 'It's a jack, and a big one at that. Think you can hit it?'

'Well stop this crate and let me see.' Jason stepped down and pulled out his gun. He took careful aim and pulled the trigger. The rabbit scampered off and disappeared before Jason had a chance for a second shot.

Wes had to laugh as he came down beside him. 'You shoot that thing like an old lady. Hell, boy. All's you need to do is just clear leather and shoot. You don't need to think about it. Let your hand do the thinking. Let me show you.'

The two boys spent half an hour drawing and shooting until Jason ran out of bullets. Once they got back into the wagon, they put the horses into a trot to try to make up some time. Once in town they pulled the wagon up in front of the mercantile, gave the horses some water and went inside.

'Mornin', Toby,' greeted Wes. 'Miles sent us to pick up some supplies for the XO. Says you have some posts and wire for us.'

Toby had his back to the door as he busied himself with a display of canned goods. When he turned to see Wes and Jason crossing the threshold, he pointed a boney finger at Jason and began to come toward him. 'You young whelp, you git out of my store,' he shouted. 'You're not welcome in here. You're a little red headed demon and I don't want you in my store!' He began to push Jason toward the door, but Jason would have no part of it and began to push back.

'You little hellion, git out of my store

now,' cried Toby as he continued to shove Jason toward the opening. 'I said 'git out'!'

The lone townsman in the store ran out the door and headed toward the sheriff's office.

Wes stepped forward and tried to intercede. 'Hey you two, knock it off.' He turned to the tradesman. 'What's gotten into you, Toby?'

'This ain't none of your concern, Wes. You stay out of this,' insisted Toby as he and Jason continued to scrap. Finally, Jason had had enough of Toby pushing and insulting him. He let loose with a hard right hand to Toby's stomach and doubled him over, then gave him a couple more blows to the head that put the man on the floor. He pulled out his revolver and pointed it at Toby. Then, remembering the pistol was empty, he put it away.

Wes grabbed Jason and pulled him off before he did any more damage. 'What the hell are you doing, Jason? What the *hell* is the matter with you?

You pulled your gun on him. This is not good, no sir, this is not good at all.'

Just then Sheriff Joe Mason came through the door. He was a big man, a good head taller than any other man in town and an ex-army officer to boot. When he gave an order, people took heed. He grabbed Jason by the front of his shirt and stood him up against a post. Putting his other hand to Jason's throat, he cautioned him. 'You stay right here and don't move a muscle.'

He let go of Jason to tend to Toby. Jason spoke up. 'He started it, I . . . ' The sheriff grabbed him by the shirt and slammed him up against the post a second time, harder than before; almost knocking the wind out of him. 'I told you not to move a muscle, and that includes your mouth!'

The lawman went back to checking on Toby. When he was satisfied Toby was all right, he asked Wes to take him over to see the doctor. 'I think he needs a couple of stitches over that left eye.'

Wes and Toby headed out the door

and Sheriff Mason turned his attention toward Jason. He took his gun from him and motioned toward the door. 'Pick up your hat. Let's go.'

Jason stood his ground. 'Go, go where? I didn't do anything. He started it, I was just defending myself.'

'Shut up! You're going to take a time out until I can get the facts on this little episode. Now move out.'

Jason was still reluctant to move. 'You're going to put me in jail for this?'

Fed up with the boy's stubbornness, Mason was having none of it. He lifted his right foot and gave the boy a nudge with the toe of his boot. 'Well, I ain't going to buy you a drink, that's for sure.' He paused at the doorway just long enough to hang up the 'closed' sign and shut the door behind them.

★   ★   ★

Wes and Toby went into the doctor's office where Sarah met them.

'My goodness, what happened, Mr

152

Tobias? Let's get you right in here where Doctor Dunn can take a look at that cut.'

Sarah began to get the utensils ready as Ben began to examine the cut on Tobias. 'So, what happened here, Toby? Did you take a fall?'

'No, I didn't take no fall. That red headed devil hit me.'

'Red headed devil?' Sarah asked, obviously confused. 'I'm afraid I don't know who that is.'

'Oh, yes you do,' Toby declared bitterly. 'That son of Satan XO boy, the little red-headed bastard! The sheriff hauled him off to jail.'

Sarah slapped Toby across the face and ran out the door.

'What the hell was that for?' he questioned as he rubbed his cheek.

'That 'son of Satan' is Jason McKinney, her son,' Ben answered.

'Oh, I see.'

Sarah ran over to the sheriff's office. Sheriff Mason had just finished locking up Jason as she came through the front door. 'What are you doing putting him in jail like this? You let him out right this instant,' she demanded.

'Ma'am?' Mason couldn't help but smile as he faced the attractive and petite woman.

'You heard me, let him out; this has got to be some kind of mistake.'

The lawman shook his head. 'There's no mistake, ma'am. I locked him up, and until I find out why he beat the tar out of Andy Tobias, locked up is where he'll stay. And just who are you to him?'

'I'm his mother,' Sarah declared flatly.

Mason swiped his hand across his upper lip, hiding the smile. 'Well I guess that explains your irrational behavior. I am sorry, ma'am, but he stays put until I sort this whole thing out.'

'Go back to work, Ma,' Jason shouted through the bars of the holding cell. 'It's all a big mistake.'

'That sounds like good advice, ma'am,' Mason said softly. 'There's nothing you can do here.'

Sarah turned and left in a huff. By the time she arrived back at the office, Ben had finished stitching up Toby's cut and she met him at the door as he was leaving. He stopped and looked at her, expecting to receive an apology for being slapped, but when he realized none would be forthcoming, he continued on his way, mumbling under his breath.

Wes followed Toby back to the mercantile. 'I still need to pick up those supplies for the XO.'

'You'll get no supplies from me today, young man. You go back and tell your boss if he wants his supplies he'll have to come get them himself.'

Wes played contrite, hoping for an end to the foolishness. 'Oh come on, Toby. I didn't have anything to do with this.'

'You was with him. That's enough for me. So it's like I said, if the XO wants its supplies Miles Hanley hisself will have to come and get them. Now git!'

Wes left the mercantile and started for home. He had plenty of time to think and no matter how he laid it out in his mind, there was no way Miles was going to be happy with what he had to tell him.

When Wes pulled up into the front yard it was half past three and Miles was waiting on the porch. Wes felt instantly sick in the pit of his stomach as soon as he saw his boss.

Miles stood up from the chair he was in, leaned up against the post at the top of the stairs. He took a puff of his pipe. Wes sat in the wagon waiting for the questions he knew were about to fly his direction.

'I thought I told you to be back here by noon?' Questioned Miles. 'Where are my supplies and where's Jason?'

'Well, sir. I know you told us to be back by noon, but we ran into a bit of a situation.'

Concerned, Miles looked up. 'Situation? What sort of a situation? Is Jason all right?'

'Well, yes, Jason's all right, but he's in jail.'

Miles started down the stairs. 'Get

down off that wagon, son. You've got some explaining to do, and it better be good.'

Wes did as he was told, but stayed close to the wagon. 'Well, it's like this. We went straight into town just fine, but when we went to talk with Toby about our supplies, he came unglued at Jason, for no good reason I could tell. Those two got to tusselin' and Jason up and hit him. That's when the sheriff got involved. He took Jason off to jail until he could get the matter figured out.'

Miles took a deep breath. 'And what about my supplies?'

'Well, Toby wouldn't let me have them. He say's you have to come in to town and pick them up personal like.'

'What! Why do I get the feeling there's more to this story than what you're telling me?' He raised his hand, stopping Wes's answer, and shook his head. 'I think I've had just about all I want from Jason. Now that Little Walt is up and about again, I think it's time I cut that boy loose. Go into the bunkhouse and gather up his belongings. Put them into the wagon along with his saddle. Then tie his horse to the back. Looks like I'm making a trip into town.'

Wes hesitated a bit, upset with himself for having let down his employer. He finally spoke up. 'You want me to come along with you?'

'No,' Miles answered. 'You've wasted this day. You might as well lay low for what's left of it. I'm docking you a day's pay.'

'What!' Wes bit his lip, turned away from Miles and took a swooping kick at the dirt, kicking up dust as he headed across the yard. Miles could hear him cursing all the way to the bunkhouse.

As soon as Jason's belongings were loaded up, Miles headed into town. He only hoped he could get there before Toby closed up for the evening. Miles really hated to do this to Jason, but he had a business to run and it had nothing to do with babysitting. Jason was turning out to be more than he bargained for.

158

The rancher made good time and managed to reach town before Toby had shuttered the store. Entering the mercantile, he was surprised to see the storekeeper with a large gauze bandage wrapped around his head. He tried to put on a good face in spite of the situation.

'Good afternoon, Toby.'

'Good? What the hell's good about it?' Toby vehemently replied.

Miles knew right away this was not going to be a pleasant conversation. 'I understand one of my boys took a swing at you this morning.'

'Took a swing at me? He damn near killed me. I've got sore ribs and a cut on my head that took seven stitches to stop the bleeding.'

Miles acted surprised. 'Really? I heard different. I guess I was misinformed.'

'Yes sir, I guess you were. Did your informant tell you why he 'bout killed me?'

'Wes said you went crazy, trying to push Jason out of the store as soon as they walked in.'

'That's right. And do you know why that is?'

'No, I'm afraid I don't,' Miles answered, not really caring.

'It's because I sold him a gun the other day and he didn't like the price I was askin'. On his way out, he spit all over my glass display case and left me to clean up the mess. He's a disrespectful, hot headed little runt and I won't ever allow him in my store, ever again, ever!'

'I can understand how you feel toward the boy, Toby. I hope you don't feel that way about all the boys at the XO? In fact, I'd like to give you my personal apology. You just let me know what the expenses are for any damages and for the doctor. I'll make it right. If it makes you feel any better, I'm on my way over to the sheriff's office right now to let the boy know that he's no longer working for the XO.'

Toby relented. In the back of his mind was the thought that Miles could afford to shop elsewhere if so inclined, and it tempered his response. 'Well yes, that makes me feel a whole lot better. Maybe that little whelp will leave town and never come back. That would suit me just fine.'

'I still need to get my supplies, so don't close up before I get back,' Miles cautioned.

'Why, I'd be more than happy to load up those supplies myself. I'll have 'em in your wagon before you get back,' he promised.

* * *

Miles untied Jason's horse and grabbed up his belongings. He led the horse down the street to the sheriff's office, tied it to the hitch rail out front and stepped inside. The sheriff was busy at his desk and Jason was lying on the cot in one of the cells.

'Afternoon, sheriff,' greeted Miles as he stepped in.

'Well, good afternoon, Miles. Come to pick up your boy?'

Miles dropped Jason's belongings onto the floor. 'Not exactly.'

'I see.'

Jason heard Miles and got up off the cot. 'Miles, are you here to get me out? It's all a big misunderstanding.'

'Jason, I've had enough of your short temper. I put up with it for a while, hoping you'd grow out of it, but it just keeps coming. You're through working for the XO. I'll give the sheriff here your back pay. I'll even pay your bail. When you leave here, don't come out to the ranch, you're no longer welcome.' Miles pulled some money out of his pocket and handed it to the sheriff. 'This should cover it. If it's too much, give the rest to the kid.' He walked over to Jason for a last word. 'I'm sorry things didn't work out, Jason. Really, I am. You seem to be a good kid; it's just that you've got a short fuse and a bad temper. If you don't get it under control, things could go really bad for you. I hope you can work it out. Take care.' He turned away, leaving Jason hanging against the bars. As he passed the sheriff he softly commented, 'Don't let him out until I'm well out of town.'

'He'll be here for a few more hours,' replied the sheriff.

After Miles had left the office, the sheriff moved Jason's belongings away from his desk. As he did he noticed the axe handle sticking out of his rifle scabbard. He pulled it out to examine it. Jason stood watching.

'Why do you carry an axe handle, son.'

'Because I don't own a rifle.'

'You don't own a rifle and your gun has no bullets. Other than a hot temper, I would guess you were pretty harmless, until now. This stick looks like it has blood on it.'

'It does.'

'And just whose blood is this, if I might ask?'

'It belongs to my ma's husband. I beat him half to death before we rode out on him. It was repayment for all the times he beat us.'

163

'Are you sure you only beat him *half* to death?'

'Go ask her yourself,' Jason challenged. 'She's right across the street at the doctor's office.'

'I think I will,' replied the sheriff as he walked out the door, stick in hand.

As he stepped into the office, Sarah was busy filing some papers. 'Miss McKinney, or should I say, Mrs. McKinney?'

She turned to see Sheriff Mason standing in front of her with an axe handle in his hand.

'Excuse me, Mrs. McKinney, but I have a question to ask you.'

Ben heard the sheriff talking with Sarah and stepped into the room. 'Is there a problem here, Sheriff?'

'Oh no, no problem. I just have a question to ask Mrs. McKinney about this here axe handle. It was in with Jason's belongings Miles Hanley brought by my office earlier.'

'Belongings?' questioned Sarah. 'Why would Miles bring Jason his belongings?'

'Because Jason no longer works for

the XO. Miles cut him loose.

'What! Miles fired him?' Sarah began to cry. Ben put his arm around her and tried to console her.

'I'm sorry ma'am, but I need to ask you a question. Jason tells me he beat your husband half to death with this stick before the two of you left home. Is that correct?'

Sarah stopped crying and dried the tears from her eyes. 'No, Sheriff Mason, that is not correct. The day Jason and I left Topeka, I beat my husband half to death, not Jason.

Mason was unable to hide his surprise. 'You did? Not Jason?'

'Yes, Sheriff, that's correct,' replied Sarah, her voice trembling. 'My husband was a drunk, and when he drank he got mean. Jason and I endured his beatings for over ten years. One day I couldn't take it any longer. As he was about to beat Jason, I thought, 'No, this isn't going to happen anymore.' The axe handle was by the door, so I grabbed it up and went out into the yard. I came up behind him and swung it as hard as I could, hitting him over the head with it, but I'm afraid I didn't stop there. Thinking he might turn on me, I beat him until he couldn't get up and then we gathered a few of our belongings and rode off. He was alive when we left him. At least I think he was.'

'Let me see if I have this right. You beat your husband senseless and then just rode off and left him,' reiterated the sheriff.

Trembling, Sarah nodded her head. 'I couldn't take it any longer. I needed to get us out of there.'

'Even so, I'm afraid I'm going to have to wire Topeka and see if there have been any charges filed against you.'

'I did what I felt I had to do, Sheriff, I'm sure you'll do the same. I'll be anxious to hear the reply. When will you be letting Jason out of your jail?'

Mason nodded, not completely satisfied with the situation. 'His bail's been posted. He'll be out within the hour.'

'You let me know, I'll come get him.'

5

Good News, Bad News

After the sheriff left, Sarah slumped down into the chair behind her desk, clearly in distress. She leaned forward, propped her elbows into her lap, and buried her face in her hands.

'I knew this would catch up with me eventually,' she cried. 'Ben, I'm sorry you had to hear all the sordid details of my miserable life. Jason and I were terribly abused at the hand of that tyrant. I'm afraid he'll come looking for us, and I'm worried about what he might do if he finds us. I don't think Jason needs to worry about him any longer. He's grown up so much over these past few months, I'm sure he would fight back, but if Jim finds me, he may just kill me. I know I wasn't much of a mother to Jason, I've always loved him like my very own son, but I've never been able to protect him the way he needed to be. And look at him now! He's in jail and so full of anger and resentment. I can't control him any longer, Ben. I don't know what to do. I'm sorry if I'm becoming a burden to you. If you want me to leave, I'll understand.'

Ben had been setting on the edge of Sarah's desk, letting her carry on, but at the mention of her willingness to leave, he had to speak up. 'Leave, why would I want you to do that? You're perfectly welcome to stay on here. If you think I have a problem with your past, you're sadly mistaken. Seems to me, you redeemed yourself and took a bit of retribution on your way out the door, and from the sound of it, I'd say it was well deserved. Why don't you wait and see what the sheriff comes up with before you make any rash decisions.

'I'll let you in on something, Sarah. Something I've been wrestling with myself as of late. I received a telegram

168

several weeks ago. It was from my father back in Richmond. He believes it's safe for me to come home.'

Sarah didn't think she could feel any lower, but with this bit of unwelcome news, she discovered it was truly possible. She cared for Ben and had dreamed of a day when they might be able to have a relationship that was more than cordial. Now those thoughts seemed to be slipping through her fingers in the same way her son Jason was slowly slipping out of her life.

'But Sarah,' continued Ben. 'You may be happy to know that I've decided to stay here, in Fort Scott.' Sarah lifted her face fromher hands and Ben wiped the tears from her eyes as he continued to speak. 'As long as you're here I have no desire to leave, and only good reasons to stay. I know you're a married woman, Sarah, and I'll respect that, but it doesn't change the fact that I care for you. Would you please allow me to help you through this pain you're feeling right now?' He stroked her long brown hair. 'I know there are happier times for you just over the horizon. Please, give me the chance to get there with you. My guess is that Jason won't want to stay here in Fort Scott for long. He'll be moving on and you won't be able to convince him otherwise. You'll need a strong shoulder to hang your head on and I want to be there for you.' Sarah stood up and gave Ben a big hug. 'Thank you, Ben. You're a true friend. I most truly need a shoulder right now and I would be more than delighted to have yours.' She kissed him lightly on the cheek and separated herself from their embrace. 'Would you accompany me to the sheriff's office while I retrieve my son?'

'It would be my pleasure.'

Ben placed a sign on the office door 'Be back soon' and the two of them walked over to the sheriff's office.

As they entered the office, Sarah announced, 'Sheriff Mason, I'm here to pick up my son.'

'Well, I'm obliged to deliver him to

you, ma'am,' replied the sheriff as he walked over to the cell door and unlocked it for Jason. 'Seems you're living under a silver cloud at the moment, son. Toby has refused to press battery charges against you. You're free to go, but I suggest you don't leave town, you or your mother, at least not until I hear back from Topeka concerning the beating of Mr McKinney. If he's pressed charges, or worse, if he's dead, we'll be talking again. Either way, I don't want to have to go far when I come looking for you.'

'And how long will that be?' inquired Sarah.

'I expect I'll hear something by tomorrow,' Mason answered.

'I'll pay for a couple of rooms at the boarding house until this is cleared up,' offered Ben.

'That'll be fine by me,' replied Jason. 'Where might I find my horse?'

'I believe it's tethered out front,' answered the sheriff. 'Did you hear what I just told you, son, about staying close?'

'I heard you,' Jason replied. He

turned to his mother. 'I'm taking my horse to the livery for the night. I'll catch up with you and Ben later.' As he began to pick up his belongings, he realized the axe handle was missing and turned back to the lawman. 'I'd like my axe handle back, if you don't mind.'

'I'll be holding on to that for the time being. You can have it back tomorrow, if the word I get from Topeka allows it,' replied the sheriff.

Jason was clearly unhappy with the whole situation. He picked up his gear and headed out the door to retrieve his horse. Sarah and Ben followed close behind.

'I'm obliged to you, Ben, for covering the cost of our rooms,' stated Jason. 'I don't understand why he wants us both to stay in town. I told him I was the one who beat Jim, not you.'

'I told him different, Jason. I told him I beat Jim, not you. This is my cross to bear, not yours.'

Jason's jaws tensed, and he stared hard at the ground for a long moment.

'I swear, if he's still alive, and you end up in jail over this, I'll kill him as sure as I'm standing here.' He untied his horse and headed toward the livery.

Ben hollered out, 'Come back to my office in a couple hours and I'll take you and Sarah to get some supper.'

'I appreciate the offer, Ben. You're a good man, but I think I'll be taking my supper at the boarding house tonight. Take Ma out, she'll appreciate it.'

'Suit yourself, but if you change your mind, come on by.'

Jason took his horse to the livery where he rubbed him down and fed him. Ben and Sarah walked over to the boarding house and paid for two rooms, then walked back to Ben's office.

After Jason had taken care of his horse, he went over to the boarding house and retrieved the key to his room. It was on the second floor. He went up the stairs, went in and closed the door behind him. The room was small. It had a single bed next to the room's only window. A nightstand next to the bed held a single lamp. Next to the door was a stand with a bowl and pitcher of water for washing up. Jason threw his saddle-bags onto the bed, and stood in front of the window looking out to the street below. It was late and the sun was giving off its last rays of light. He could see the mercantile down the street. Toby was just locking up. The gauze bandage on his head shown white below his hat and his long dark shadow stretched almost across the street. *Damned old man*, thought Jason. *Hope your head hurts for a month of Sundays.*

Turning back to the bed, he sat down and began to go through his bags, hoping nothing had been left out, and trying to determine what he might need when he left town. Reaching into one of the bags, he felt a small package and pulled it out. It was a box of cartridges with a note attached to it that read, 'Can't defend yourself without bullets. I know you're out. Good luck. Wes.'

Jason had to smile. He hadn't done that in a while and it felt good. He had made friends with the men at the XO, and thought about the day Ira had bought him his first drink and how they all had a good laugh at his reaction. His smile quickly disappeared as he realized he'd more than likely never see any of them again. Taking the bullets, he loaded his gun and spent the night locked in his room, repeatedly drawing the gun from its holster and trying to decide what to do with the rest of his life.

When Ben and Sarah got back to the office, her concern turned toward her brother, Mac. 'I need to get a message to Mac somehow and let him know I'm all right. He'll be worried if I don't show up tonight.'

It was almost time to close the office and Doc Evans had already left for the day, so Ben offered to close up a bit early and ride out to Mac's place to let him know what was going on. Supper together would have to wait for another day.

As Ben rode out toward Mac's place, he had time to think about the decisions he had made lately. His father was upset about his not wanting to return to Richmond. His mother on the other hand knew the country and understood perfectly why he had made the decision to stay, or so she thought. He remembered times as a child, when she would long to be back in the wide-open spaces. She talked about Kansas like it was something to behold. He never gave it a second thought, but now that he was here, there was a total understanding of what his mother was feeling at those times when she would reminisce. And now, his practice with Doc Evans was off to a good start and there was plenty enough work to keep them both busy. His personal life had taken a turn as well, and there was someone in his life that he had strong feelings for, regardless of the fact of her current marital situation. He had no intention of taking advantage of the woman — that would be lower than low

— but he was going to do everything within his power to convince her that she was deserving of something more that a loveless marriage to a man who had deeply hurt her. 'She can find an attorney in town and file for a divorce,' he thought, knowing she certainly had grounds. But to bring that up to her wouldn't be right. It would have to be her decision to end their marriage agreement, not his.

The sun was about to set as Mac's house came into view. The few clouds in the summer sky showed a vestige of red and pink around the edges, and a soft glow of lantern light showed through the front window. Mac must have heard Ben's horse coming up to the house as he opened the front door before the man was even off his horse. 'Dr. Dunn, what brings you out here this evening? Is everything all right? Where's Sarah?'

'Good evening, Mac. Everything is fine. I've just come out to deliver a message. Sheriff Mason ordered her and Jason both to stay in town this evening. It's a long story. May I come in out of the cold and relay it to you?'

Without hesitation, Mac stood back and gestured the man forward. 'By all means, do come in.'

The two men spent the better part of an hour talking about Sarah, Jason, and the situation as it presently stood. As the discussion ended, Ben had a much better understanding of Sarah's past, and as Mac became more familiar with Ben, he, too, had shared some of his own story. Opening up, Mac confided that he was pretty distraught by the fact Jason had not taken to him, but he was also smart enough to understood just why that was. Between the two of them, it was concluded that Mac needed to take Jason's aloofness in his stride. He had enough to worry about just trying to make the payments on his land. Mac told Ben that Miles Hanley had agreed to sell him one of their prize bulls and that that would go a long way in helping him build up his herd.

'A cattle broker with no cattle to buy is a sad state of affairs,' reflected Mac. 'But with this new bull I may be able to hold things together.'

It was plain to Ben that Mac was resolved to make the best of it and was earnestly working toward building up his own herd while periodically buying and reselling small herds of longhorns that deviated off the Chisholm. He openly confided to the doctor the cattle were more than likely cut from larger herds along the way to Abilene or Wichita; and probably by men of unsavory character. But Mac was in survival mode and was able to buy them cheap and sell them quickly for a profit, so few questions were asked. It was clear Mac was good with bookwork as well as the logistics of getting the animals to a buyer quickly, before suspicions were aroused. And although Mac liked the doctor — perhaps was even beginning to trust him — he was careful as to just how much he shared, and skillfully avoided divulging too much.

As Ben rode back to town that evening, he reflected on his circumstances and the situations of those around him. Sarah and her brother, Mac, were good people; much like himself in the fact that life had dealt them a bad hand and starting over was not an easy task. And even Jason, with his hot temper and tendency to make bad decisions, was a good kid deep down. The boy just needed a few more years to gain the maturity necessary to survive out here in the west. Back in Richmond, survival of the fittest meant being adept in business practices and shrewd in financial decisions. If you didn't have that ability, you were destined to spend your days as a lower class citizen, but out here it was different, out here in Kansas, survival of the fittest was more primal. Everyone was after the same thing, survival; period.

He liked the fact that neighbors helped neighbors and everyone pitched in to give each other a helping hand whenever it was needed. Miles didn't have to sell Mac one of his prize bulls. He could just as easily stood back and let Mac go under opening up the opportunity for the XO to expand their land holdings, but he didn't. And Mac didn't hold a grudge against Miles for his involvement in the blockade of the Shawnee.

Ben had learned that the Shawnee had been closed off some twenty years earlier due to the cattle from Texas carrying a disease that Kansas cattle couldn't overcome. Opening the trail again after the war was a bad idea. Mac didn't see it that way and took advantage of the situation, but the ranchers and farmers in Kansas and even into Missouri would have nothing to do with it. It took them close to a year to close it again, and the XO played a big part. It cut Mac and others off at the knees. Most didn't survive, but Mac held on. 'He's a survivor,' thought Ben. '*And Miles understands that.*'

Ben had grown quite happy with his situation out here in the wide-open plains of Kansas and felt his decision to stay was a good one. Now that he had made up his mind to become a permanent resident of Fort Scott, there were a few things he needed to take care of, but most importantly, he needed to be sure there would be no charges brought against Sarah for the beating of her husband.

The following day Ben opened up the office to a chilly morning. A slight breeze made it seem colder than usual, but then it was October, and Fall was definitely in the air. Sarah showed up late and went right to work as Ben and Doc Evans discussed business in one of the other rooms. As their meeting finished up they came out to the reception area where Sarah was busily filling out a backlog of paperwork.

'It's so nice to have you working here, Sarah,' complimented Doc Evans. 'Ben's idea to hire you was first rate. In fact, since he's been here, we've almost doubled our number of patients. He's building up quite a reputation for himself, and for this office I might add. Without you here giving us a hand with all the paperwork and assistance with patients, we'd never be able to manage.'

Sarah's smile was timid, but heartfelt. 'Well thank you so much for the compliment, Doctor Evans. It's nice to be appreciated.'

'Well you have a wonderful day now, dear. And that goes for you too, Ben. I'm off to see Mrs. Simmons about an infected foot. I'll eat well tonight, as she has little money, so I barter with her for a couple of chickens whenever I visit.'

As he left, Ben turned his attention to Sarah. 'And how are you doing this fine chilly morning?'

Sarah didn't look up and continued to work on her papers. 'I'm sorry I'm late, Ben.'

Ben reached out, gently cupping her chin and forcing her to look up. 'Don't be sorry. I'm surprised you're here at all.'

She sighed and leaned back in her chair. 'I need to stay busy. I'm so nervous about what Sheriff Mason might hear, I can hardly stand it. What if Jim's pressed charges against me, or worse, what if he's dead? I might go to jail. Do you think they might hang me?'

Ben shook his head. 'Sarah, I think any judge in his right mind would let you go in a heartbeat once the truth of what that man did to you and Jason came out. Personally, I doubt if any charges will be forthcoming. I just can't imagine he'd want the world to know what kind of person he really is.'

Sarah couldn't fully shake the feeling of dread, but Ben's faith gave her solace. 'I hope you're right, Ben. I really hope you're right.'

He resisted the urge to kiss her, patting her cheek instead. 'I have every confidence that things will work out in your favor today. I've adjusted my schedule to keep myself in town, but right now I've a few errands to run. I should be back before noon.'

Ben slipped out the door and headed to the telegraph office where he planned to send a message to Richmond. As he stepped inside, he was greeted at the counter by a cheerful young man, probably not much older than Jason. Behind the counter at a small desk where the clicker was, sat an older man, the boy's father, listening intently as he turned the constant clicking sounds into decipherable messages.

'It never ceases to amaze me how someone can take the clicking sounds from that little pad and turn it into a full blown message,' commented Ben.

'It's quite amazing, I have to agree,' replied the boy. 'I've heard that some day we may even be able to talk into a little box and actually have our voice be heard by someone at the other end of the line.'

The old man finished his writing and turned his attention toward his son. 'Impossible,' he interjected. 'That'll never happen. You can't send a human voice over a wire.'

'When you were my age, Pa, did you ever think you'd be sitting here sending and receiving messages from little electric impulses?'

'Well, no, but that's my point,' the older man blustered. But he was inwardly proud of his son's fanciful musings. 'These are electrical impulses, not a human voice.'

The young man at the counter turned his back to his father and rolled his eyes, ignoring the comment. 'And what can I do for you today, Doctor Dunn. Your usual weekly telegram?' he asked.

Speaking loud enough for the older man to hear, Ben replied. 'Even though it once seemed impossible, I'd like to send a telegram to my father in Richmond.'

The young man smiled and played along. 'All the way to Richmond, Richmond Virginia?'

The older man quickly caught on to the game they were playing and interjected, 'See that there box on the counter. Why don't the two of you try yelling your message into it and see what happens!'

Ben and the young man began to laugh. 'I'm sorry, sir,' Ben apologized. 'Your son and I were just funnin' you. We meant no disrespect.'

'I take no offence,' replied the older man as he went back to receiving another message.

Ben handed the young man a slip of paper with the message he wanted sent. 'Would you please read it back to me? I want to be sure I have it right.'

The boy nodded, pleased that he had been asked. 'I'd be happy to. Let's see, to 'Mr Nathanial J. Dunn of Richmond, Virginia, *Father, I have received your message and am delighted to hear that the way has been cleared for my safe return. You may not like the reply I am sending, but after much aforethought and anguish, I have made the decision to remain here in Kansas. Tell Mother I now understand her occasional longings for the place of her birth. Please send the remainder of my belongings in care of Miles Hanley, XO Ranch, Fort Scott, Kansas. Your son, Ben.'* How does that sound?'

Ben nodded his approval. 'That sounds perfect. Please let me know when you receive a reply.'

'I'm glad to hear you'll be staying on,' called the young man as Ben left the office.

His next stop was at the local land office. The clerk, a middle-aged man with long sideburns and a big mustache was bent over a drawing laid out on a table behind the front counter. A short cigar balanced on the edge of the table filling the room with a haze of blue-grey smoke. Without looking up, the clerk asked, 'What can I do for you?'

'I'd like to discuss purchasing a piece of property from you,' Ben answered.

Without straightening up, the clerk turned his head toward the counter to see who was speaking. Recognizing Ben, he replied, 'Well, Doctor Dunn, come back around here and take a look at this.' He turned back toward the drawing.

Ben walked around the counter to have a look at what the clerk found so fascinating. Laid out on the table was a street map of Fort Scott. It showed more streets than actually existed. 'This here, Doctor Dunn, is the future of Fort Scott. I've been commissioned by the town's governance to draw up plans for its expansion. Did you realize our fair city has over four thousand souls living within its boundaries? Bonds have been recently passed for the grading of new streets. We're expanding quite rapidly, and you, sir, are one of the first to see it on paper. And since you're here to discuss the purchase of property, you have your pick of the litter.'

Ben was no fool. He was from Richmond where his father had made a fortune in real estate speculation. He knew an opportunity when it was presented to him so he studied the map closely.

'I see here that the town will be expanding to the north, along the railroad line and to the west, away from it.'

'Yes, that only makes sense, otherwise the railroad would eventually run right through the middle of town,' the agent agreed.

His arms folded against the table, Ben was still studying the map. 'And when will these properties be available?' *There was no way he was going to point out any specific plots.*

'Why, they became available just this morning,' the salesman smiled.

'Just this morning?' Ben asked. 'And these parcels that are already blocked out?

The man cleared his throat. 'Well, I'm afraid those parcels are already taken. Our town council had the opportunity to view this drawing last night as they voted on the passage of this plan, and, well, you know how it is with politicians. They always seem to find a way to benefit themselves.'

Ben laughed. He had grown up at his father's knee learning the ins and outs of real estate wheeling and dealings. 'I understand that all too well, I'm afraid. However, it does look like they did leave a few nice parcels, especially these here, toward the north along the tracks.' Ben pointed out six parcels that were next to each other and still open. 'These look like they're in the business district?'

'Yes, they are. These are one quarter acre plots and these other parcels to the west are for housing, they're one acre each.'

Ben used his finger to point at the map. 'And what would the price of these six parcels in the business district, and this one parcel right here in the housing area, cost me?'

'These six here? Well, let me see.' The clerk ran a few calculations. 'Those six combined encompass a total area of one and a half acres, and if we add on the one acre plot, that come to a total sum of seven hundred dollars.'

'Seven hundred dollars for two and a half acres?' Ben countered. 'That seems a bit steep, don't you think?'

'This is city property, Doctor Dunn. Not open range.'

'It still seems a bit steep, but I see your point. Draw up the appropriate paperwork and I'll pay you in cash; and be sure to draw up a receipt for payment as well.' Ben considered himself a fortunate man, as he was about to capitalize on all his father had taught him.

The transaction took longer than expected and by the time Ben left the land office it was close to noon. He hurried back to his office but Sarah wasn't there, so he made his way to the sheriff's office where he found both Sarah and Jason. 'I'm sorry I'm late. What has the sheriff found out?' He stood behind Sarah and Jason, who were sitting in chairs in front of the sheriff's desk.

Mason was leaning back in his chair with his feet on his desk and a cocky grin on his face. The axe handle was in his hand and he repeatedly tapped it on the edge of his desk. He looked like a schoolmaster ready to scold a couple of unruly students.

'I'm not really sure this concerns you, Doctor Dunn,' he grinned, obviously enjoying himself.

'Ben is a good friend and my employer,' answered Sarah. 'He stays.'

'Very well,' he replied as he began to explain the details of his inquiry. 'I sent off a telegram yesterday to the sheriff in Topeka, looking for information on the beating of Mrs. McKinney's husband a little over six months ago. What I found out was very interesting. The damage was severe. A concussion, three broken ribs, a broken arm, two broken fingers and an assortment of cuts and bruises. I must say, Mrs. McKinney, you're a woman not to be tangled with when your dander is up. And yes, I did verify that you were the one who wielded this here axe handle, not your boy. You're very lucky you didn't kill the man, but I do believe you may have taught him a lesson he'll likely never forget. Up to this point he's not pressed charges so you're both free to go.'

Sarah heaved a huge sigh of relief as Jason leaned over the desk and grabbed hold of the axe handle. Looking the sheriff in the eye, he stated, 'I believe this is mine.'

The sheriff dropped his feet to the floor and stood up, still holding the handle. 'Son, you have a chip on your shoulder and a healthy disrespect for the law. That's a lethal combination that'll get you no further than the end of a rope.' The sheriff jammed the handle forward, striking Jason below the sternum and knocking the wind out of him. Jason grabbed at his stomach and the sheriff let go of the stick and it fell to the floor. 'Get him out of here,' he ordered, as he sat back down.

As the three of them headed for the door, the sheriff called out. 'Oh, by the way. I got my information from a Doctor Brown. Seems your husband has recently disappeared. Retribution can be a terrible thing. I'd watch my back if I were you.'

The three of them walked out to the street, Ben seemed relieved 'Thank God, that's over.'

'Over, what are you talking about,' cried Jason. 'You heard the sheriff, Jim's disappeared. I doubt if he's holed up somewhere, he's probably heading this direction and I aim to find him before he finds us.'

'You have no proof of that,' Ben declared.

'Proof, I don't need proof. I know the man,' Jason retorted.

Ben shot back. 'Even if it is true, and he is heading in this direction, just how do you plan to stop him?' Beside him, he felt Sarah tense and tightened his grip on her arm to reassure her.

Jason was in full rant. 'I'll look in every saloon between here and Topeka if I have to. He's a drunk! He'll be in one of 'em. There's no doubt about that.'

Sarah had remained quiet as she mulled everything over in her mind. Finally, she spoke up. 'Jason, please don't do anything foolish.'

Jason shook his head at the woman's entreaties. 'He'll kill us if he finds us, you know that. I'm not about to sit back and let that happen.' He kissed his mother on the cheek and headed to the boarding house to pick up his belongings.

Ben tried to assure Sarah that everything would be all right, but she wasn't so sure.

'Why don't you head back to the office and I'll try to talk some sense into him.'

Sarah agreed, and as she headed back to the office, Ben followed after Jason.

He caught up with him at his room. The young man had already strapped on his gun and was busy loading up his saddle-bag.

'Jason, you know this could be a fool's mission. If he doesn't kill you, you may end up killing him.'

Jason continued to pack. 'That's the way I want it, Ben. I'd love to see that old man lying in a pool of blood, looking up at me and knowing exactly why he's about to meet his maker. I hope he begs me for forgiveness. So help me, I'll gut shoot him, spit in his face and watch him die. And then I'll piss on his grave!'

Knowing it was useless to continue, Ben shook his head. 'I promised your Mother I'd try to talk you out of this,' he said. 'But since it appears I can't, is there anything I can do for you?'

Jason was surprised at the offer, but decided to accept. 'Yes, as a matter of fact, there is. Toby won't let me in his store and I need a few supplies. If I give you a list, will you get them for me?'

Grimly, Ben nodded. 'Let me have the list. I'll meet you out front, or maybe right around the corner, so he doesn't see you.'

Jason wrote out a short list of supplies and handed it to Ben, who proceeded to the mercantile where he purchased them. As Tobias added the supplies to a sack he couldn't help but wonder why Ben would want such items. 'Let's see, hard tack, matches, beans, coffee, a box of .44s. I didn't know you even owned a gun.' He eyed the doctor suspiciously. 'If I didn't know better I'd say you were heading out of town for a spell.'

Ben was counting out the appropriate amount of gold and silver coins. 'Tobias, you have no clue, and it would be best if it stayed that way. Thank you for the supplies.' Without another word, he picked up the tote and headed out the door.

As Ben stepped down on to the boardwalk, he reached into his vest pocket and pulled out what folding money he had on him and added it to the sack. Going around the corner he found Jason, mounted and waiting. He handed him the sack and watched as Jason tied it to the saddle horn.

Ben reached up, laying a hand on the boy's knee. 'Be careful, Jason. And let your mother know you're all right whenever you can. She'll be worried about you.'

'Tell her not to worry. I'll be fine.' Jason spurred his horse and disappeared down the street.

As Ben turned to head back to Sarah, he saw Tobias standing on the walk. 'Well, I for one am tickled to see that little red headed demon leave this town.'

'Go to hell, Tobias,' replied Ben as he walked on by.

6

Trailing the Dog

Jason headed west along the same route
he took with Mac and Sarah when they
came to Fort Scott earlier in the year.
His first stop would be Fall River. There
were a few small encampments between
Fort Scott and there, mainly used by
drovers who had brought cattle up from
Texas. Some of them were more
interested in seeing this part of the
country rather than heading straight
back home. Most of them headed
toward the west, but for those heading
east, Topeka, Fall River and then Fort
Scott was where the trail took them.

He was hoping he would meet up
with Jim along the trail somewhere and
not in Fall River. He traveled cautiously, always keeping his eye on the
trail ahead. The first day didn't get him

too far as he had started out late in the afternoon. He decided to make camp just before dark, next to an outcrop of large boulders shaded by one old cottonwood tree; as the rocks would afford him some protection against the cold night breeze. After taking care of his horse's needs, he gathered what wood he could find from the trees downed branches and built a small fire. Grabbing up the sack of supplies Ben had purchased for him, he opened it looking to see what he could find to eat and was surprised to see that Ben had also added a cut of bacon. He continued pulling out the supplies to see what else he might find when he came upon the money Ben had added to the sack. He was pleasantly surprised to find that Ben had added twenty dollars toward his travel expenses.

After eating his fill of beans and hard tack, and drinking a whole pot of hot coffee, he was tired and his bladder was full. A short walk away from the fire to relieve himself suddenly made him realize just how cold it was. He gathered a few more pieces of wood and piled a few rocks close to the backside of the fire in order to reflect a bit of heat and hold some warmth through the night. After stoking the fire he leaned his head against his saddle and covered up with a single wool blanket. Under the twinkling stars and the soft crackle of a warm fire on a cool October night, Jason slept soundly.

The following morning he awoke to a fire that, except for a few small coals, was all but out. Some dry grass saved from the night dew and a few breaths of air was all it took to get a new flame. He reached for a couple of sticks from the pile he had gathered the night before, but quickly pulled back. There on the pile laid a King snake. They weren't usually active at night especially in October, but the fire must have warmed the rocks where he was hiding enough to bring him out. Jason grabbed up the axe handle from its scabbard and clubbed it to death. 'Breakfast,' he thought as he began to skin it.

After eating and drinking his fill of hot coffee, he doused the fire with what was left, and then packed up camp. Today would be a full day of riding and the following would bring him to Fall River.

It was about noon when Jason first saw him, a rider heading his direction. He was too far away to make him out clearly, so caution was essential until they got closer to each other. Jason's heart was pounding harder with each step closer to the stranger. Thoughts were buzzing through his head. *What if it's him? Do I just shoot him and be done with it, or do I say something, and then shoot him? What if he recognizes me first?* He pulled his hat down low in front, put his hand on his pistol and thumbed back the hammer. The stranger was no fool to caution. He raised his hands and shouted out, 'Just passing, not looking for trouble.' Jason stopped and hollered back, 'Pass on by, and just keep your hands where I can see them.'

As the stranger got closer, Jason realized it wasn't who he was looking for. A feeling of both relief and disappointment filled him.

'You're a mighty cautious kid,' commented the stranger as he came alongside. 'Thanks for not blowing me out of my saddle.'

'Didn't mean to scare you,' replied Jason, pulling to a stop. 'I'm half expecting to meet someone along this trail that would just as soon kill me as see me. Where are you coming from?'

'Fall River yesterday, Topeka before that.' The man pointed to his shirt pocket, and then took out his makings, rolling a smoke. He offered the tobacco to Jason.

Jason declined the offer of a smoke. 'Are you from Topeka?'

'Originally from Laredo, Texas, but I spent several months in Topeka once we sold off our cattle.'

'You didn't happen to hear of a man named McKinney, Jim McKinney, while you were there, did you?' He reached out, patting his horse's neck; calming the animal.

'McKinney, hmm, name doesn't sound familiar, but there's a lot of people in Topeka.'

'He hung out in the Trails End saloon.'

The man laughed. 'I've been there a time or two.'

'He drank a lot, and usually lost at the faro table. Does that sound familiar?'

'A lot of people drank too much and lost at the faro table. Why hell, I'm guilty of that myself. What else you got?'

'He might have been favoring a leg, like it had been broke recently.'

The cowboy stroked his chin. 'Now that does bring somebody to mind. I haven't seen him in a few weeks. Last I recall he was booted out of the Trails End for beating up on one of the women that worked there. The bartender paid off a couple of the boys to take him out back and gave him a shellackin' as payback. I figure he's holed up somewhere while he licks his wounds. Does that help any?'

'It sure does. Thanks for the information. How much further to Fall River?'

'Over a day's ride yet. Ride till dark, get an early start in the morning and you should be there by mid afternoon easy. I spent a few days in Fall River. Nice little town, but stay clear of the poker table. There's a man in there from down south, around the delta area I believe. I swear he cheats, He wins way too often, but he's too good to get caught at it.'

'Much obliged. Say, are you heading into Fort Scott by any chance?'

'That would be my next stop.'

'Would you mind finding a Doctor Dunn's office and relaying a message for me?'

'No, not at all.'

'There's a woman at the reception desk named Sarah. Tell her Jason's doing fine.'

'"Jason's doing fine", that's it?' the man echoed.

'Yeah. Sarah's my ma, she'll be worried, so if you forget my name, mention my red hair. She'll know.'

'Got it. You take care now.'

'And you as well.'

Jason and the rider parted ways and he rode on without incident, only stopping toward dusk to make camp. It was a long cold night. The following morning a thin layer of frost blanketed the ground. Jason built up the fire to warm himself and heat up what was left of last night's coffee. He ate a meager breakfast of bacon and hardtack soaked in the fat. After packing up, he headed on toward Fall River. It was a cold morning ride, but the sun finally did show itself enough to warm things up and make for a pleasant afternoon.

It was early evening when the town first came into view. Upon arriving he stopped in front of the only diner. After watering his horse, he tied it to the hitch post and went in. His breakfast was long gone and hardtack wasn't appealing to him at the moment. His mind was set on a hot meal. The diner was quaint and tidy. Red and white checkered table clothes were neatly laid out and adorned with dried flowers. The cook was a middle-aged man; clean-shaven and what looked to be a new haircut. He wore an almost clean apron.

Taking a seat at a table next to the window, the waitress promptly and politely took Jason's order of steak and potatoes, two biscuits, hot coffee and a slice of fresh apple pie. The meal was served quickly and he took his time eating while watching the goings on outside the window. Sheriff Brass was talking to his sister, Ellie in front of her store, which reminded him to see about buying a warm jacket before he left town. As soon as he finished dinner, Jason got up and took the two biscuits with him. After paying for the meal he stepped outside and fed the biscuits to his horse, then led him across the street to the general store. Stewart was just about to close up when Jason walked in. He had to do a double take before realizing who it was.

'Well I'll be danged, Ellie, come on out here and take a looksee, you'll never in a million years guess who just darkened our door.'

Ellie stepped out from the back room. 'Why, I'd know that shock of red hair most anywhere. Jason McKinney, how the heck are you, son? How's your momma doing?'

'Ma's doing fine. She's got herself a real job in a doctor's office.'

'Well good for her. I'm real happy to hear that. So tell us now, what brings you to Fall River, son?'

'I came by to buy a jacket. It's getting mighty cold out there at night.'

'You came all the way to Fall River just to buy a jacket from us,' laughed Stewart jokingly. 'Well bless your heart. So are you planning to stay awhile or are you just passing through?'

'I'm on my way to Topeka, if I need to go that far.'

'If you need to go that far?' questioned Ellie thoughtfully. 'You're lookin' for someone, aren't you? Is it that no good skunk . . . what was his name again, Jim?'

Jason nodded. 'Fraid so. Word is he may be on his way to Fort Scott, looking for me and Ma. I figure on finding him before he finds us. Have you seen any strangers in town lately that might be walking with a limp? He more than likely would be hanging around the saloon.'

Ellie and Stewart both thought about it for a moment. 'No, no, I don't believe we have. We've had a lot of drovers coming through here lately after they bring their cattle up from Texas. Most stay in Abilene or head back down south, but some decide to stick around to see this part of the country. Can't say as we've seen anyone with a limp though.'

'I think I'll try my luck at the saloon. Maybe someone over there might know something. I'll stop by in the morning to pick up a jacket and a few supplies before I head out.'

'Have you got a place to stay the

night?' asked Stewart.

'I plan on getting a room. As long as I'm in town I might as well sleep in a warm bed. I'll be back in the morning.'

'You're welcome to stay the night here, son.'

'I appreciate the offer, but I may be out late. I think I'll just get me a room.'

'Suit yourself, can't say we didn't offer.'

Jason walked his horse over to the livery and bedded it down for the evening, then made his way to the boarding house where he rented a room for the night and stowed his gear. He had a few extra dollars in his pocket and thought as long as he was going to be at the saloon, why not try to make a few more at the poker table.

By the time he left the boarding house the sun had set, and even though he had never been in the saloon, the town wasn't that big, so he didn't think he'd have much trouble finding it. There were a couple of side streets off the main, and the first one he tried turned out to be the correct one. The sign out front read 'Fall River Saloon'. 'This must be the place,' he thought to himself.

He entered cautiously so as not to bring notice to himself and slowly surveyed the room. It was small and dimly lit. A stairway to the left led up to the second floor and the bar was straight ahead. The bartender looked up long enough to get a good glimpse of his newest customer, and then went back to busying himself behind the bar. There were four tables. Two had games in progress and two sat empty. At one of the games sat a man who Jason thought might be the fella he was told about, and three men stood at the bar. There was no piano, so other than the talk of the men inside, it was fairly quiet. After satisfying himself that Jim wasn't there, he headed for the bar. Anticipating his next move, the bartender met him as he walked up.

'What can I do fer ya, young fella'?' he asked.

'I'll have a beer.' Jason didn't normally drink beer, but he was hoping to get in on a game and didn't want to dull his sensibilities with whiskey. He could nurse the beer as he sat at one of the empty tables, waiting for an opening at one of the games. The bartender poured him a beer and Jason paid the man, then went and sat down. There was a deck of cards on the table, so he occupied himself by shuffling and cutting them for lack of anything better to do.

After about a half an hour one of the men at the card shark's table jumped up in disgust. 'I've had it, you've cleaned me out. There's no way in hell a man can win that many hands and not be doing something fishy.'

The gambler just smiled. 'I beg to differ with you, sir, I seem to be doing everything right. That's why I have all of your money,' stated the shark. 'Are you accusing me of some sort of underhandedness?'

'Well, I won't go that far, but I'm

done for the night. I won't be sittin' in on a game at your table again.'

'If that's the way you want it, that's fine with me.' He looked over in Jason's direction. 'Hey, kid. Interested in sitting in? We seem to have an open chair.'

Jason was hoping for an opening at the other table, but at the invitation thought, *Why not, how good can this guy be?* 'Sure, I'll fill in,' he replied.

As Jason got up, the man just leaving the game walked by his table on the way toward the door. 'Watch him,' he whispered. 'I don't know how he's doing it, but somehow he's cheatin'.'

Jason walked over and introduced himself all around.

The game had been going for about an hour and Jason was holding his own. He had won a few hands and was feeling confident. *This guy isn't that good,* he thought to himself. But not too soon after, the tide began to turn in favor of the shark and the majority of the bets were flowing his way. After the shark had won a close hand with one of the other players, the loser jumped up and demanded to see inside the shark's jacket.

'You're cheatin', mister. I don't know how you're doin' it, but I know you're not playin' fair. Now stand up and take off that jacket so I can see what you got up your sleeve,' demanded the player.

'I'll do nothing of the sort,' replied the shark.

'The hell you won't.' The player drew his gun, but before he had a chance to take aim, a shot rang out. The player grabbed his arm and spun to the floor as the shark stood up, holding a smoking gun in his hand. The players gathered up their money, as the game was obviously over.

Somebody ran for the sheriff and before long, he arrived along with another man who turned out to be the doctor.

'Don't anybody leave,' he ordered.

Jason stood back and watched as the doc checked the man who had been shot. He was still alive and able to walk.

The doctor took him out as the sheriff began to question the shark. After he was through with him, he turned his attention to one of the other men who sat at the table, then soon turned his attention to Jason. As he looked at Jason, a sudden realization came over him.

'Well I'll be damned, if it isn't the red headed runt. Didn't I once tell you to leave and not come back?'

'No, you told me not to look back.'

'And if I'm not mistaken, I believe you did. Just what brings you back to Fall River, Red? And if you say two hundred dollars, I'll lock you up and lose the key.'

'I'm just passing through on my way to Topeka.'

'And trouble follows you wherever you go, don't it,' remarked the sheriff sarcastically.

'It ain't following me, I'm looking for it.'

'Oh, still a smart ass, are you?'

'No sir, just stating a fact.'

'Well here's a fact for you, son. Plan on being out of town tomorrow morning before the sun comes up, and if you should happen to find any more 'trouble' between now and then, I'll surely lock you up, understand?'

'Perfectly, May I go?'

'Please do.'

Jason left the saloon and headed back to his room at the boarding house. He'd come away from the table five dollars ahead.

The following morning, Jason was up early, but not as early as the sheriff had suggested, as he needed to pick up a jacket and a few supplies before he headed out. As he stared out the window of his room, contemplating how he could skirt around the sheriff, he noticed a rider coming into town from the west. The man pulled up in front of the general store and slowly dismounted. Watching the rider tie his horse and walk around the hitch rail to the boardwalk, Jason thought he had detected a limp. At first he thought his eyes were just playing tricks on him. He continued to watch the man as he stepped up onto the boardwalk and made his way to the door Stewart had just opened. As he walked into the store, it became clear that the man indeed had a limp.

Forgetting the fact that the sheriff might see him, Jason strapped on his gun and headed toward the store. He didn't know for sure if this was the man he was looking for, but there was only one way to find out. As he reached the store, the sheriff saw him from his office.

'That damn kid. I told him to be out of town by now.' He grabbed up his hat and headed toward the store.

As Stewart was setting out some of his merchandise onto the boardwalk, he noticed the rider coming down the street. As he headed back inside, Ellie, who had also seen the rider, watched him tie up just outside. 'Stewart,' cried Ellie in a hushed voice. 'That man outside. He has a limp.'

As the stranger came inside, it was plain to see that the man had quite a pronounced limp. Ellie busied herself straightening a display in front of the counter as Stewart greeted the man.

'Good morning, sir. How may I help you?'

'You can git me a blanket,' he ordered. 'It's colder than the dickens out there. I 'bout froze to death last night. What time does your saloon open up around here? I need a drink to warm my bones.'

'That would be in about thirty minutes,' replied Stewart.

'Where 'bouts are you coming from?' questioned Ellie.

'From Topeka, if it's any of your business.'

'Topeka? And where are you heading?' Ellie was folding and refolding a piece of dry goods, pretending to make pleasant conversation.

'Why the hell is that any of your business?' the man snapped.

Stewart interjected. 'Now see here, mister. You better be careful how you talk to my wife.'

'Or what? You're a skinny old man. I got nothing to fear from you.'

'Well I ain't so skinny,' stated Ellie, as she stepped up to the man, her eyes narrowing. 'And you darn well better fear me.'

Stewart, anticipating trouble, quickly went behind the counter to retrieve an old scattergun he kept there.

'I fear no woman,' the man replied. 'I've beat down meaner women than you.' He gave Ellie a shove and she grabbed hold of him by the shirt. He backhanded Ellie, but she wouldn't let go.

Stewart had the gun pointed at the stranger and was ready to pull the trigger as soon as he had a clear shot. 'Let her go, mister, or I'll blow you in two,' he yelled.

As the two scuffled, Jason walked in the door. He pulled his gun and cocked back the hammer.

'Jim' he shouted out.

Turning to see who had called his name, the man realized it was Jason and went for his gun. Jason didn't hesitate to pull the trigger, hitting Jim in the chest. He put two more slugs in him before he fell to the floor.

Sheriff Brass came through the door just as Jason fired. He pulled his gun and leveled it on Jason.

'Jonathan, don't you dare,' shouted Ellie. 'He just saved my life.'

Sheriff Brass put away his gun as Jason walked up to Jim who lay on the floor in a pool of blood. He was breathing hard. Looking up at Jason, he said, 'You shot me, son.' He actually sounded surprised.

Jason looked down at the dying man, and with contempt in his voice, growled, 'I was never your son. I was only your whipping boy. You don't know how often I've dreamt of this day.' He spit in the old man's face, not one bit of remorse in him as the old man's eyes closed for the final time.

Stewart hugged Ellie. 'Are you all right?'

'I'm fine,' she replied as she stepped over to Jason and gave him a hug.

'Thank you for saving my life.'

'Believe me, Ellie. It was my pleasure.'

'I thought I told you to be out of town before sunup,' stated the sheriff. 'For once, I'm glad you didn't listen to me. So, this is the man that gave you and your mother so much grief, is it. I'm going to need to write up a report on this.'

'Am I under arrest?'

'No, you're free to go. What would you like done with the body?'

Jason thought about it for a long moment. 'Bury it, I suppose,' he murmured. 'And the sooner, the better.'

Jason went back to his room and stayed there the rest of the day. The following morning he packed up his belongings, walked over to the livery, settled up and saddled his horse, then walked over to the telegraph office and sent a message to his Ma. 'Jim's dead, I'm fine,' was the extent of the message. From there he went to the general store. Ellie and Stewart were busy as always when he walked in. The first thing he noticed was that the blood had been cleaned up.

Stewart greeted him as he entered. 'Young Jason, how are you doing? What can I do for you this morning?'

'You can sell me a warm jacket and some supplies for starters.' After Jason found a jacket to his liking, Stewart filled a sack to the brim with supplies. 'No charge,' he stated with a smile as he handed the sack to Jason.

'No charge? Well, thank you.'

'Our treat for saving my life,' replied Ellie.

'You know he wouldn't have killed you,' Jason admonished. 'He took his pleasure from beating on women, not killing them.'

'I know, but as long as Jonathan believes it, that's all that matters. Do you recall the promise I made to your mother when you were here last? I told her that if that no account showed up here in Fall River, I'd make sure he didn't go any further, and I keep my promises. So, are you heading back to Fort Scott?'

'No, I think I'll go on to Topeka and maybe head south before the snows come. I'd like to see a bit more of this country before I head back. Will you do me a favor and get a message to my ma. Let her know what all happened and that I'm all right.'

Ellie nodded. 'I'll do that for you, Jason. I promise.'

As Jason McKinney headed out of town he stopped at the pauper's field where a fresh grave had been dug. He rode up to it and dismounted. Pulling the axe handle from its scabbard he stuck it into the fresh dirt, not at the head of the grave, like a headstone, but in the center, like a stake through the heart. He found a rock and pounded it in securely, then remounted his horse. As he sat there looking down at his handiwork with a satisfied grin on his face, he spoke but one word. 'Bastard.' He then spurred his horse and headed west, toward Topeka.

7

Money Trail

Just days away from his sixteenth birthday, Jason McKinney had already killed three men. The first out of necessity and the second was purely unintentional, but the third, the third was out of pure and unrefined hatred. It didn't bother him in the least to put a bullet in the man that had caused him so much grief. In fact, it was the killing of the third man, Jim, which gave him the most satisfaction. To know he or his ma would never have to be looking over their shoulder, wondering if or when they would meet up again, took a load off his mind.

As he headed out of Fall River he realized that for the first time in his life he was truly free. Free to do whatever he pleased. 'Why go straight to Topeka,' he thought. 'Why not head south and see for myself where all these longhorns are coming from.' With winter coming on, Jason really had no desire to be spending any more time than necessary out in the cold, so he turned south and headed toward Texas.

For most of the day he found himself riding through tall grass, but being October, the new green shoots waving in the summer breeze were long gone, replaced now by brown and broken spent grass that had seen better days.

It was late afternoon when he came upon them. At first he wasn't sure what he was seeing. Maybe it was a herd of buffalo, but then again, maybe not. As he got closer he realized it was a small herd of longhorns, maybe two hundred head or so. They weren't moving, but it seemed too early to bed them down for the night. He was soon close enough to analyze the situation more clearly. Only two drovers could be seen, and they were toward the back of the herd. There was also no remuda. Something didn't seem right. His instincts told him to avoid the men, but he rejected it and rode up to where they were standing.

One of the men drew his gun as Jason came close. One was older; the other was a young kid about his age. Trail dust covered their clothes and they seemed a bit disoriented, almost out of their element. 'What can we do for you, son,' questioned the older man who held the gun on him.

'Just passing by, I'm not looking for trouble. You look shorthanded. Are the two of you trying to move these cattle by yourselves?'

The two drovers looked at each other as if communicating without saying a word. A smile came across the younger kid's face and the older one put away his gun. 'We had close to eight hundred head until yesterday morning. We were overtaken by a group of maybe twenty men. They shot several of us including our wrangler. The remuda was taken along with most of our cattle. The boy and I are all that's left. We managed to round up these few head that scattered during the ruckus, but we're having a hard time moving 'em along with just the two of us.'

'If you're heading to Dodge City, or even Topeka, you're heading in the wrong direction.'

'We're not going to either. We have a buyer in Fort Scott and we're heading that direction. He was expecting eight hundred head, but he'll have to be satisfied with what we can give him.'

'Fort Scott you say? Who's your buyer?'

'I don't think that's any of your business, but I'll tell you what, if you're interested in giving us a hand moving these critters, we'll make it worth your while, say, a hundred dollars.'

Jason knew something was up. The only broker left in Fort Scott was Mac, and his operation wasn't big enough to handle eight hundred head. Once again his instincts told him to keep moving, but the lure of a hundred dollars for a two, maybe three-day ride was awful tempting. Plus, he was curious to see just what was going on with these men and Mac.

'A hundred dollars, you say. And all I have to do is help you get these cattle to Fort Scott?'

'Yep, that's all you need to do. We're in a desperate situation right now, as you can see. With another man we should be able to do it. It won't be easy, but I think we'll manage. What do you say?'

Jason thought about it for a minute. He could easily ask for two hundred and probably get it considering the situation, but two hundred could just as easily get him a bullet in the back at the end of the trail, so he decided not to push it. 'OK, you got yourself a deal.'

'Great! My name's Jake. This here is Randy.'

'Good to meet you, I'm Jason.'

It was still light, so the three men decided to push the cattle for a few more hours. 'You two take the lead,' ordered Jake. 'I'll take drag for now, but tomorrow we trade off.'

They made a few miles headway before calling it a day and making camp. That evening the three spent huddled around the fire conversing and drinking hot coffee, as the nights were getting colder.

'So tell me, Jake,' asked Jason. 'Where did you start out from?'

Jake hesitated a bit with his answer. 'We started out around Waco.'

'How many men did you lose when your cattle were taken?'

'How many? Well let me think. We lost four . . . and one was wounded, but died later. So I guess that would be five altogether.'

'What do you think the owner of these cattle will say when he finds out most of his herd was stolen?'

All the questioning was beginning to unnerve Jake. 'What the hell are you askin' me so many questions for, boy? I don't know what he's going to say. You think I'm a mind reader or something?'

'Sorry, Jake. I was just making conversation.'

'Well I don't like the conversation, so why don't you just keep quiet!'

'Maybe I'll just call it a day and get me some shuteye.'

'That might be a good idea.'

Jason moved away from the fire and crawled under his blanket for the night while Jake and Randy sat up and whispered amongst themselves. He knew he needed to keep an eye on these two, but for now, they needed him, so he figured he was safe for the time being.

'Do you think he's on to us, Jake,' whispered Randy.

'No, I think he's just an inquisitive kid, but I can't make up answers as fast as he's asking the questions.'

'I wish Thurman was here, and then we wouldn't be needing any help from this kid.'

'Well Thurman ain't here,' scolded Jake. 'He got himself shot. We all knew the odds when we took these cattle, so stop whining.'

'Yeah, but he set up the deal in Fort Scott.'

'That don't matter. I know the name of the man we need to see, and I know where to find him. We'll do just fine. Why don't you get some sleep, you'll be pulling drag in the morning.'

'Are we really going to give him a hundred dollars of our money?'

'No, we're not. That boy will have an accident as soon as we get our money. Don't you worry about that. Now get some sleep.'

The following morning the three men were up before the dawn and had themselves a hot breakfast, then headed out at first light. They had a good lead steer with a fast pace, almost like he knew it was late in the year and was anxious to get out of the open. They made good time and expected to get to Fort Scott before the end of the following day.

That evening Jake and Randy spent a fair amount of time talking amongst themselves, and Jason was beginning to get a bit concerned about how this was going to turn out, so he started to devise his own plan, just in case these two decided to turn on him.

The following morning, Jake ordered Jason to take the drag position. Jason was happy to hear that. Now he could keep an eye on the two of them until they reached their destination.

Later that afternoon they crossed the road that led into Fort Scott and continued on north.

As they did, it just so happened that Little Walt and Smiley from the XO were out checking fence in the area, and when they heard the bellow of cows off in the distance, they decided to investigate.

'Do you hear that, Smiley?'

'Sure do, but those ain't ours.'

'Let's take a closer look.'

They rode toward the cover of a small stand of cottonwoods at the top of a small rise. Off in the distance they observed a herd of cattle moving to the north.

'Them's longhorns,' stated Smiley.

'They sure are. Do you suppose they're lost?'

'It could be possible, but they're a long way off the trail. Nobody can be that lost.'

'Well then if they're not lost, do you think they've been stolen?'

'Don't know, but I think we should let Miles know we seen 'em as soon as we get back.'

The men finished up their work and as soon as they got back to the ranch they found Miles and reported what they had seen.

'Say, Miles, Smiley and I saw an unusual sight today and we thought we should let you know. When we were out checking the north fence this afternoon we heard the bellerin' of cows off in the distance, so we decided to investigate.'

'Those wouldn't have been our cattle,' interjected Miles.

'You're right,' continued Walt. 'We got ourselves under those cottonwoods on the northern knoll and took a look. They were longhorns, about two hundred or so. They were heading north.'

'Longhorns, are you sure about that?'

'I know a longhorn when I see one,' replied Smiley. 'You know, cattle with looonnngg horns.' He opened his arms as wide as they would go while he extended the word long.

'I don't need the anatomy lesson, Smiley. Get my horse for me, would you? It looks like I have an errand to run.'

'Need us to go with you?'

'No, this one I'll handle on my own.'

Once Miles got his horse, he mounted up and headed toward town. He made it in just over an hour and went directly to the sheriff's office where Sheriff Mason was finishing up his supper.

'Well good evening there, Miles. What brings you into town at this time of the day?'

'Joe, I need your help.'

'You need my help? Is everything OK?'

'I'm thinking not. Do you recall the conversation I had with you the other day about my suspicions concerning Mac Shepard?'

'Why sure I do. You think he might be involved in some illegal activities concerning Texas longhorns.'

'That's right. A couple of my men spotted a herd of maybe two hundred, pass just west of town earlier this afternoon.'

'Longhorns, are you sure about that?'

Thinking of Smiley's answer to that same question earlier in the day, Miles couldn't help but grin before he answered, 'Yes, I'm sure. My men know longhorns when they see them.'

'Well then let me get a couple of my deputies and we'll pay ol' Mac a surprise visit.'

Meanwhile, the cattle crossed the road to Fort Scott and kept going north, passing within two miles of Mac's place. They kept moving for another hour until they came to a spot not far from the railroad tracks. Jake had them hold the cattle up there.

'You two stay here and watch these

cattle. I'll be back by evening,' stated Jake.

'Why didn't we take these cattle into Fort Scott? Why did we pass it?' questioned Jason.

'If you ain't got this figured out by now, you're dense in the head, boy.'

'What, that these cattle are stolen.'

'He's got us figured out, Jake. What are we going to do now?' cried Randy.

Jake looked over at Jason. 'You still wantin' a hundred dollars?'

Jason knew better than to say no. 'Yes sir. It don't matter to me whose cattle these are as long as I get paid for helping you move them.'

'Does that answer the question for you, Randy?'

'I suppose it does. But what if you ain't back by tonight?'

'Quit your worrying, Randy. I'll be back.'

The sun had set by the time Jake reached Mac's place. He came up to the back of the house and dismounted, tying his horse to a tree in the yard. He

walked around to the front of the
house, went up to the door and
knocked.

Mac opened the door to see a very
dirty stranger standing on his front
porch. 'Can I help you?'

'Yes, you can. Thurman sent me.'

'Thurman? Come with me.' Mac
walked Jake out away from the house as
Sarah was inside and he didn't want her
to hear what was being said.

'Where's Thurman, and who are
you?' questioned Mac.

'Thurman's dead, I'm his partner,
Jake. He gave me your name and told
me how to find you before he died.'

'You have the cattle at the rendezvous
point already?'

'Yes, we wouldn't have made it at all
if we hadn't picked up this red headed
stray along the trail. He gave us a hand
getting them here.'

'Red headed kid? What's his name?'

'His name, it's Jason, why, you know
him?'

It's a good thing the two men were

238

standing in the dark, as the look on Mac's face would have shown through his answer. 'No, just curious. I wasn't expecting you to be here until later this evening. All the arrangements have been made. But the railcars won't be in place for a couple more hours, so just sit tight. We'll load as soon as they show up and then I'll pay you. If they show up before I get there, start loading.'

'We'll do that, but I'm not letting them leave until I get my money.'

'Fair enough.'

Jake mounted up and rode off into the night and Mac went back into the house to get things ready. 'Jason,' he thought to himself. 'How in the hell did he get himself mixed up in this? That's it. When I get rid of this bunch, I swear to the almighty, I'm not going to do this again.'

It had been close to an hour since Jake left and he was just about ready to leave himself when there was another knock at the door. Mac opened it to find Sheriff Mason and Miles Hanley standing just outside.

'Good evening Sheriff, Miles, This is a late hour to be calling on people. I take it this isn't a social visit. What can I do for you?'

'May we come in out of the cold?'

'Why yes, where are my manners, please do come in.'

Sarah, who was sitting in the front room, stood up. She had gotten the telegram from Ellie in Fall River telling her of her husband's death as well as the details of how it happened, and that Jason was heading south to 'Sow His Oats' as she put it. But seeing the sheriff and Miles made her think otherwise. She disliked Miles for firing her son and she disliked the sheriff for the way he had treated her and Jason. She wanted to leave the room, but her intuition told her otherwise.

'Is it Jason, is he all right?'

'It's not Jason, ma'am, this concerns Mac.'

'Me?' inquired Mac. 'How so?' All Mac could think about was to stall them as long as possible. 'Sarah, would you mind putting some water on the stove. It's cold outside and I'm sure these two men would like to warm up some after their long ride out here.'

Sarah went to get some water. She took her time as she was grateful to be out of the room, even if for only a couple of minutes.

'Please, have a seat, what's this all about?'

'Mac, I don't know how to put this, and please understand, I'm not accusing you of doing anything against the law, but I need to know upfront, are you still buying and selling Texas longhorns?'

Mac knew they had suspicions. Why else would they be here at this late hour, but the accusation was made, and he needed to put up a good front as well as stall for time.

'Well for one thing, Sheriff, and you too, Miles, it's not against the law to buy or sell Texas longhorns, but ever since the Shawnee was blockaded, there haven't been any cattle up from Texas to do either. I'm sure you know all about that, Miles, since the XO had a big hand in it. My guess is that you weren't too concerned about Texas fever as much as you were about the influx of beef cattle in the area lowering the price of your own herd. And now the two of you have the gall to 'accuse' me of doing something that is perfectly legal?'

'Mac, you're taking this all wrong,' replied Miles. 'We're not accusing you of doing anything wrong, but you're right about no longhorns coming into Fort Scott, so when my men see a herd of close to two hundred of 'em heading this direction, I have to wonder if they've not been cut from a larger herd and being sold illegally.'

'So tell me, Miles. Did you see any Texas longhorns in my corrals when you rode up here this evening? Did you see any fresh sign of two hundred cattle on my property? Did you?'

'No, can't say as I did. But you're the

only one left around these parts who may still have connections to buyers back east, so it only makes sense that we would come here first, don't you agree?'

'Well you've come here and you've made your accusations. I'm sure you've had your look around and realized there's nothing to see. So if there's nothing else you wish to accuse me of this evening, I'd say we're through?'

Just then Sarah entered the room, 'The tea water is hot.'

'Well, thank you ma'am, but I think we'll pass on the tea this evening if that's all right with you,' replied the sheriff. 'Mac, sorry to have bothered you, let's go, Miles.'

Miles and Sheriff Mason headed out the door and onto the front porch. The sheriff headed for his horse. His two deputies stood outside blowing into their hands and stomping their feet, trying to keep warm. 'Did you see anything, men?' the sheriff called out.

'Not a thing, Sheriff.'

'Then head back to town, this has all been a big misunderstanding.' He mounted up and turned to Miles. 'There's nothing illegal going on out here, Miles. You've drug me and my men all this way for what? Nothing! If you're boys did see longhorns pass by here, they're probably in the next county by now and that would make them none of my concern. I'm going back to town, Miles. Don't even try to apologize. I ain't in the mood.' He turned his horse and rode off to catch up with his deputies.

Miles, on the other hand wasn't ready to give up so easily. He still had his suspicions and decided to ride down the road a ways and watch the house. If Mac was involved, he'd be leaving soon enough. All he would have to do is follow him.

After the two men left the house, Mac sat on the edge of his chair and gave a big sigh of relief.

'What was that all about?' asked Sarah.

'I'll explain it all to you later. Right now I need to run an errand. Don't wait up for me.'

'An errand this late at night? What's going on here, Mac?'

'I'll explain it to you later. Right now, I think Jason may be in trouble.' Mac grabbed his gear and headed for the door.

'Mac, what do you mean, Jason may be in trouble? Stop right now and explain this to me.'

Mac turned back toward Sarah. 'Not now,' he insisted. 'I'll explain it when I get back. If anyone comes to the door, don't tell them a thing.'

He hurried out to the barn and saddled up his horse. Miles was watching and as soon as Mac left the barn, he began to shadow him.

By this time, the boxcars had shown up and the men began to load the cattle. Jason and Randy counted as they ran them into the cars.

'That Mac best be showing up here is short order. It's like I told him, I ain't letting this train go until I get paid.'

Once the cattle were loaded, the engineer began to shovel coal into the burner.

'Hold off on that, buddy,' insisted Jake. 'You ain't going anywhere until I get paid.'

'I don't have your money mister, but I do need to get this train out of here.'

'You may not have my money, but you have my cattle, and I ain't been paid for 'em yet. So you're going to sit tight until my money shows up.'

Jason interjected. 'Jake, let him go. If you keep him here, we could all get caught. I'm good for the money. Let him go.'

'What are you talking about, boy, 'You're good for the money.''

'You said Mac, Mac Shepard, right?'

'Ya, Mac Sheperd. How did you know that?'

'Mac Sheperd is my father. Let the train go and you can hold me in exchange for the money.'

'How do I know you ain't lying to me?'

'Because I got a stake in this too. And I ain't about to go to jail just because you don't trust my father.' Jason pulled his gun on Jake and Randy, then yelled to the engineer. 'Get this thing out of here, and be quick about it.'

'She ain't quite ready yet,' he replied. 'I need another five minutes.'

'Well don't waste one second. When she's ready, go.'

Mac could hear the train in the distance, he knew he was late and only hoped that the men had loaded the cattle. Miles heard the train as well. It didn't take much thinking to figure out what was going on. He needed to catch them red handed, and not get himself killed in the process.

Jason ordered Jake and Randy to drop their guns. When they did, he collected them and ordered the two men onto their horses. When they were all mounted, he ordered them to ride away from the tracks. As they rode, he tried to explain to Jake. 'Listen, if Mac is late he has a darn good reason. We need to be out of the area in case the sheriff is wise to us. You'll get your money, I'll guarantee you that.'

Finally, the train began to inch forward, slowly picking up speed as it headed down the track. Once it was out of sight, he handed Jake and Randy their guns back. Jake pointed his at Jason. 'You may be a fool, but I'm not. Give me your gun and we'll wait for your old man to show up.'

Jason handed Jake his gun.

'Now we'll wait, and if he don't show up soon, we're all heading to his place. If he don't have my money, his house will make one hell of a bonfire, and the two of you will be in the middle of it.'

After about five minutes, Mac arrived. The train was well out of sight, but the silhouettes of the three men could be seen against a moonlit sky. As he rode up closer to them, Jake called out, 'Who goes there?'

'It's Mac Shepard,' came the reply.

'My cattle are long gone, but I got your boy. I want my money, now!'

'A deal's a deal, I'll pay you. How many head did you load?'

'One hundred and ninety,' shouted Jason.

'Two hundred even,' replied Jake.

'That ain't right and you know it. Randy, how many did you count?'

Randy looked over at Jake, who gave him the evil eye. 'Two hundred even,' he replied.

'You liar! You counted one ninety, same as me.'

'I counted two hundred even,' Randy shot back.

'It doesn't matter,' interjected Mac. 'I wasn't here to count, so we'll go with two hundred, even.'

Mac took the money from his pocket and counted out what was owed. 'Hold back a hundred for my wage,' ordered Jason.

Mac pulled back a hundred dollars and handed the rest to Jake, who put away his gun and pocketed the money. 'Nice doin' business with you, Mac. Until next time.'

'There won't be a next time,' came a voice from out of the shadows. Miles Hanley rode forward with his gun drawn.

'And what fool is this who thinks he can hold all four of us in the dark of night?'

'His name is Miles Hanley,' answered Mac. 'Just what do you think you're doing out here, Miles?'

'I'm hauling you all in for selling stolen cattle.'

'Don't be ridiculous, Miles,' replied Mac. 'Do you see any cattle here? And even if you did, how do you know they were stolen?'

'Why else would you be out here exchanging money in the middle of the night. I heard the train, and I can still smell the cattle.'

'I think you're mistaken, Miles. Those are buffalo you smell, and we're out here exchanging money because these two men are holding my son, Jason, for ransom and I'm paying them off. You've got no proof otherwise, so why don't you put down that gun and let these two men leave me with my son.'

'That isn't the way it is, and you damn well know it,' Miles countered.

'I know you'll be making a big mistake if you try to pursue it, so once again, I suggest you back down and forget this,' Mac advised. It was clear from the tone of his voice he meant business.

Miles thought about it for a few seconds. 'You're a thief in my book, Mac Shepard. You and your son. You can forget about that bull I was going to sell you. In fact, you can forget about any help from the XO. If you go under, you go under, and there'll be no tears shed by me.' He put away his gun, turned, and rode off.

Mac looked over at Jake and Randy. 'I suggest the two of you do the same.'

Jake handed Jason back his gun and the two men rode off. Mac looked to Jason. 'Let's go home, son.' And they rode off toward the ranch.

'Sarah's worried sick about you. Don't tell her about the cattle. I do like the story about you being held for ransom, so let's stick with that, all right?'

'Well it's the truth, sort of. By the way, you owe me a hundred dollars.'

Mac pulled the money out of his pocket and handed it over to Jason.

8

Moving On

As Mac and Jason rode back, they had a chance to talk some. 'This isn't the way I wanted you to know me, Jason. What I did was wrong, but it was either that or lose my ranch. I figure sometimes a desperate man has got to do desperate things to hold onto what he has, and I was desperate. I almost got caught this time, so I'm making it my last.'

'This time? You've done this before?'

'A time or two,' Mac admitted, laughing.

'You don't seem like the type of person that would do something like this.'

'I didn't think so either, Jason, but one thing led to another and before I knew it, I was caught up in it and making some really stupid decisions, and well, here I am.'

'You know, Mac, aside from everything else that's happened tonight, what I really want to know is how did you manage to get a train?'

'The engineer and I know each other. He owed me a favor, plus, he made some good money tonight. Look, Jason, I know what I've done is wrong, and I don't know what you think of me right now. You and Miles both have every right to be mad at me, but like I said, I was desperate. I didn't know how else to get the money I needed to keep my place.'

'This may not be the way you wanted me to know you, Mac, but it's too late for that. This is how I know you. I won't hold it against you, but just don't expect me to be any better and we'll get along just fine.'

'I'd like you to be a better man than me. But I won't expect it if you would rather I didn't. Listen, Jason, I don't know what your plan is right now, but why don't you think about hanging around here for the winter? I've got plenty to keep you busy.'

'I just might take you up on that. It's getting too cold around here to stay out at night.'

Once back at the ranch, they took care of the horses and headed up to the house. 'Remember what I told you,' Mac reminded Jason as they walked in through the door. Jason barely made it over the threshold before Sarah got hold of him. She pestered him with a million questions most of the night until he couldn't take it any longer. As soon as he had the opportunity to excused himself, he took it and went to bed.

After Jason had left the room, Sarah talked with Mac. 'I don't know what the truth is, Mac. I don't believe a word about Jason being held for ransom, but I don't think I want to know the truth either. I'm just glad he's back home safe.'

Jason and Mac both laid low for most

of the winter, busying themselves around the ranch. Ben had been out a few times to visit with Sarah, and she insisted on traveling into town to work. During the worst part of the winter she stayed at the boarding house in town. Mac didn't get the bull he wanted from Miles, but the two he had, kept themselves busy and when spring calving came around they added a healthy number to the herd.

It was late spring on a Friday afternoon. Jason was getting restless and needed to get away from the ranch. He decided to head into town for the weekend. A card game was on his mind as well as a drink or two.

When he arrived, he stopped in at Ben's office to see Sarah before heading over to the Hoof and Horn. As he entered, Sarah was busy at her desk. She was surprised and delighted to see him.

'You sure seem to be in a good mood today,' commented Jason.

'I have good news.'

'Really? What is it?'

'Ben proposed to me. We're getting married.'

'Wow! That is good news. Does Mac know?'

'No, not yet, and don't you tell him. I want to surprise him.'

'So when?'

'Later in the summer, when Ben's house is finished.'

'He's building a house?' He picked up a paperweight from her desk and played with it, tossing it back and forth before setting it back down in the exact same place it had been before.

'Yes, not far from here. It's very nice. Maybe he can show it to you when he gets a chance.'

'Well I'm happy for you, Sarah. I really am. I'm on my way to the Hoof and Horn. I thought I might play some cards. I'm glad I stopped by.'

'I'm glad you did too, Jason. Good luck with your card game.'

As Jason walked his horse over to the Hoof and Horn, he thought about Mac, and how he seemed to have turned the corner on his place. It looked like he was going to make a go of it raising cattle. He thought about how Sarah was starting over with a new husband and a new house. He was happy for both of them, but somehow, it made him feel out of place.

After tying his horse, he walked into the Hoof and Horn, Ike noticed him right off. 'Well I'll be damned. If it isn't the son of Satan himself.' Ira lifted his hands up, palms out. 'Only joking. How the hell are you, Jason? Come on up here and let me buy you a drink. Now let me see, the last time you were in my saloon you were holding the barrel of a gun up under somebody's chin.' Ira glanced over to his left.

The man standing at the bar turned his head toward the two men. 'That would be me,' replied Wiley, raising his glass. 'And I'll be keeping my mouth shut this time around.'

Jason smugly smiled in Wiley's direction as Ira poured him a drink.

'Here you go, son.'

Picking up the glass, he toasted it toward Ira. 'Thanks, you're a good man.' He gulped it down. 'I see the XO boys are here,' he commented as he looked at the corner table where a game of poker was being played. 'I don't see Wes.'

'Oh yeah, Wes. That's a whole other story. The way I hear it, seems not too long after you left town, ol' Wes decided he'd had about enough of the XO and decided to head out. He packed his bags, collected what pay was owed him and headed west, or maybe it was south. I don't rightly remember. At any rate, he rode out. Said he was tired of seeing a lot of nothin' around here and wanted to see where all those longhorns were coming from, and what a real mountain looked like. I miss ol' Wes, and I missed you too come to think of it. But now you're back. So, what are your plans?'

'My plans? Well, I'm not rightly sure, Ira. I think I want to head west, or maybe south. *I* want to see where all those longhorns are coming from, and I want to see what a real mountain looks like.' He laughed; he always did like Wes, and now he knew why. 'Thanks for the drink.' Jason turned around and slowly walked back out the door.

'Well, if that don't beat all,' Ira murmured under his breath.

Jason rode back out to Mac's place and packed his bags. As he was walking out the door he met Mac on the front porch. 'Mac, I'm leaving. I'm not going to try and explain it. I just feel the need to move on.'

He reached out his hand and Mac accepted it. 'It was good to get to know you, Mac.'

'Jason, are you sure you won't change your mind?'

'Nope, tell Sarah not to worry, I'll write.'

He mounted up and rode on past the corrals, now full of cows.

He headed west.

We do hope that you have enjoyed reading this large print book.

Did you know that all of our titles are available for purchase?

We publish a wide range of high quality large print books including:
Romances, Mysteries, Classics
General Fiction
Non Fiction and Westerns

Special interest titles available in large print are:
The Little Oxford Dictionary
Music Book, Song Book
Hymn Book, Service Book

Also available from us courtesy of Oxford University Press:
Young Readers' Dictionary
(large print edition)
Young Readers' Thesaurus
(large print edition)

For further information or a free brochure, please contact us at:
Ulverscroft Large Print Books Ltd.,
The Green, Bradgate Road, Anstey,
Leicester, LE7 7FU, England.
Tel: (00 44) **0116 236 4325**
Fax: (00 44) **0116 234 0205**

Other titles in the
Linford Western Library:

THE BADMAN'S DAUGHTER

Terry James

When Daniel Cliff arrives in Ranch Town, he discovers the settlement is caught in the stranglehold of a brutal tyrant, and refuses to take sides. That is until the spirited Charlotte 'Charlie' Wells, heir to the Crooked-W ranch, crosses his path. When she offers him the chance to help her right the wrongs being rained down on the town, he has no qualms about using her troubles to further his own ambitions. However, Charlie is no pawn in a man's game — and nobody is going to stand in her way . . .

KILL THE TIN STAR!

Jake Henry

They warned Savage not to take the short cut through Dead Man's Gulch. Too many Apaches, they said. The warning, however, failed to mention anything about Craig and Bobby Vandal. Father and son. One a cold killer, the other prepared to do anything for his boy. When Savage arrives in the Gulch, the local sheriff has Bobby locked up on a murder charge. Craig swears his son will never hang. Before long, a deputy's badge is pinned to Savage's chest, and he holds a smoking-hot Winchester in his hands . . .

BUFFALO WOLF

Colin Bainbridge

On his way out to the diggings, fate throws John Creed together with Polly Chantry, whose wagon he frees from the mud. At the diggings they meet with Timber Wolf Flynn and his Sauk wife, White Fawn, but there is no sign of Polly's father, for whom she has been searching. The two of them set out on a double mission: to find Polly's father, and acquire weapons to help the prospectors fight off the increasing threat from outlaws. Their quest leads them into the mountains, and to a frightening discovery . . .

100 GOLDEN EAGLES
FOR IRON EYES

Rory Black

Bounty hunter Iron Eyes is heading south to Mexico in search of outlaws Bodine and Walters, but is himself being hunted down by his erstwhile sweetheart Squirrel Sally. Then Iron Eyes learns that Sally has been kidnapped by landowner Don Jose Fernandez, and rushes to her aid. But Sally, Iron Eyes and the outlaws are all just pawns in a much larger game, with an enemy more deadly than they can imagine — and Iron Eyes has to use all his courage and skill to survive.

BLOOD OVER BLACK CREEK

Edwin Derek

Hoping to put his violent past behind him, Matt Crowe purchases the Texas ranch of Black Creek. It has water in abundance; but at the massive and powerful neighbouring Bar-T, the waters run dry in the summer. Protected by gunmen, its hands constantly drive herds across Black Creek range to the water-rich creek that gives the ranch its name. What can one man and two beautiful young women do against the twenty hired gunmen of the mighty Bar-T? Very little, until Crowe makes a dangerous ally of an old foe . . .